THE BELLS OF SHOREDITCH

By the same author:

TUNES OF GLORY

HOUSEHOLD GHOSTS

THE MIND BENDERS

JAMES KENNAWAY

The Bells of Shoreditch

READERS UNION

LONGMANS

London 1965

*This Contemporary Fiction edition was pro-
duced in 1965 for sale to its members only by
the proprietors, Readers Union Ltd, at Aldine
House, 10-13 Bedford Street, London W.C.2 and
at Letchworth Garden City, Herts. Full details
of membership may be obtained from our
London address. The book is set in 11 point
Linotype Georgian leaded and has been re-
printed by Northumberland Press Limited,
Gateshead upon Tyne. It was first published by
Longmans Green & Co Ltd.*

FOR SANDY

Oranges and lemons,
Say the Bells of St Clements,
I owe you five farthings
Say the Bells of St Martins.
When will you pay me?
Say the Bells of Old Bailey.
When I grow rich,
Say the Bells of Shoreditch.

Tommy Thumb's Pretty Song Book
(c. 1744)

Part One

Part One

Chapter 1

Merchant Banks assume the characteristics of the families who own them. Some are shy and dark affairs with birdcage lifts and heavy continental furniture, hawk-nosed, Napoleonic and very private indeed; others big-shouldered, twelve-bored, booming and bursting at the seams; some are gentlemen and some are german.

Smaller than Lazards, lighter than Hambros, less famous than Rothschilds, older than Wernhers, less rational than Philip Hill Higginson Erlangers, Sarsons Browne was still one of the better respected Acceptance Houses in the City. But then it was run by a most superior person, one J. T. Sarson, who might never be approached directly – not even at his flat in Grosvenor Square. There, his man Salmon opened the flat door not only to Mrs Sarson, but also to some other sophisticated women who sometimes called at five o'clock.

One evening last summer, he at once recognised the girl called Stella. He was clearly alarmed by her arrival. The sun was weak and watery outside in Grosvenor Square, where a handful of Ban-the-Bombers were wandering round and round, casting nasty glances at the aggressive shoulders of the new American Embassy, effortlessly destroying their cause with gypsy earrings and anarchists' beards.

Stella stood with her hands in her pockets. 'Stella Vass,' she said. She never referred to herself as 'Mrs'. It perhaps reminded her too closely of the restrictions of her upbringing. In Kelvingrove everybody used to be

'Mr' or 'Mrs', people ate with their elbows tucked into their sides and all the world wore cherry hats.

Salmon knew very well who she was. Not too willingly he pulled back the door and, with knitted brow, showed her through the dark hall into the sitting-room. He said, 'If madam would like to wait I'll ascertain whether Mister Sarson's in.'

'He is,' she said, but not with much confidence, almost wearily like a girl at a clinic. 'I heard him.'

'Yes, madam,' Salmon said, meaning nothing affirmative, and on spider legs withdrew. The room was much like a very expensive doctor's waiting-room, or perhaps more like the manager's sitting-room in a luxury hotel, where princes wait to make complaints and shadow kings meet shadow cabinets. Stella seemed to be familiar with it. She looked round it once, as if to confirm that it had not changed, and catching her reflection in the glass in front of the books, she looked more closely at herself, a big, dark, asthmatic girl with long legs and narrow hips; with eyes of such a dark tone of blue that they looked black, to all except those who loved her. For them, in those eyes, there was a whole, smoky city, with wynds and cobbles and men on strike and dark churches set on bright green grass.

She removed her beret and stuffed it in the pocket of her suède coat. She was right to do so: her hair was smooth, blue-black and shiny. She turned up the collar of her coat. Then suddenly she moved away as if disgusted by herself and with swift steps she walked all the way round the room – this room which had all the worst features of the tidy bachelor's flat. Magazines were laid out on a round table as they are in men's clubs

4

and on the shelves and mantelpiece there were silver boxes and expensive ornaments which had no unity, giving the room less, not more, personality. The furniture was white wood, a kind of chalked oak, except for the television set. The flat clearly had nothing to do with Sarson's wife, who preferred the country, but its neutrality betrayed their relationship. Sherry, gin and whisky had been decanted fastidiously by Salmon, and were laid on a wooden trolley. The only original note was the series of enormous paintings of fat pedigree short horns and Jersey cows dating back a hundred and fifty years.

Sarson was never particularly well dressed. His figure did not require him to take much more care than to see that the suit was reasonably cut in the first place. This evening he was wearing a plain jacket from one suit and the pin-stripe trousers from another. He emerged from the only real room in the flat, his bedroom, with its window half blocked by his roll-top desk, and he did not look friendly. In moments of displeasure he had a peculiar habit of drawing the skin tight over his nose, and stroking it with his forefinger. A big man; a cat-man; he had been skiing for a few days over Easter and he was still brown, his hair less grey than fair.

Stella by then was sitting in one of the armchairs, and stopping herself from jumping to her feet she reintroduced herself characteristically, fading in her thoughts.

'Oh help, help, help . . . I swore to myself I wouldn't start with an apology. But I've come at the wrong time, I'll bet.'

'Not particularly,' he said, looking at her straight for a second. 'I enjoyed the christening.'

'Oh no you didn't.'

He pushed back his hair and turned away from her, staring out of the window at some activity in a neighbouring flat. None of the windows overlooked the Square.

Stella bit her lip. Then, looking over her shoulder at him she said, 'It is the wrong time, I can see.'

He still did not reply, but rather as if some boring girlfriend of his wife had called, wandered over to the trolley to pour drinks. To his back, therefore, she called, 'You don't half put visiting ladies through it – no fire, no flowers, and this kind of eerie north light somewhere between doom and the dissecting room – all this and Salmon, too . . . I'm talking too much, I am. I must be the guilty party. It's the negative sins –' She suddenly said more loudly, expansively, even wildly, 'Did you know that? It's the sins of omission we regret.' And as he turned to look at her over his shoulder she said, 'Yes, I'm a gas-bag. I'm only saying I should have had the guts to come here sooner. By the by, I have an excuse . . .'

'Whisky?' he asked, quite gently.

'I have an excuse for being here, even if I have no reason. I've come to continue our talk about entering my boys for school . . . It was my idea asking you to be godfather; I don't know if Andrew said . . .'

'I'm taking it you want whisky.' He did not even say, 'you never did listen'. Memories of previous meetings had evidently been erased.

She sat back in the chair for a second and took two or three deep breaths. Then, still with her eyes on the back of his sunburnt neck, she said flatly, almost with a

6

sigh, 'Was it you who told me you'd got a wound on your shoulder blade?'

The light was dim in the corner. He held up the glasses to see how much whisky he had put in. Without turning round, he said, 'I don't remember telling you, but you're perfectly correct.'

'Is it a bullet or something like that?'

He smiled and said, 'Shrapnel, please. It's not meant to be the best sign to get a bullet in your back.' Then he gave rather a heavy, hearty laugh; a wrong sort of laugh; one that did not go with a sense of humour; one that rocked the boat.

He reached for the soda siphon. At home, he did not offer ice with the whisky for the same reason that he did not offer cigarettes. He did not approve of these things. Before he handed her the tumbler she said, 'I feel I should have on a big-brimmed black hat and maybe a bustle and a label round my neck.'

He sat down on the long stool in front of the fireplace, shifting some newspapers on to the floor. He seemed to be reading a headline in one of these, as he asked her, 'What would the label read?'

'You tell me.'

He looked up at her, then took a drink. 'Perhaps "Votes for Women",' he said, with a big, off-and-on smile, which he used in the City to keep people at a polite distance. She recognised it exactly for what it was, with a feeling close to anger.

'I thought you were going to suggest "Thou shalt not commit adultery",' she said, then blushed. He did not answer. She seemed to have difficulty controlling her breath.

She said more steadily, 'I've just jumped in the deep end. You don't know the courage it took to come here. Did you think I was going to call on you?'

'As I remember,' he said perfectly pleasantly, 'you had a date to do so. You're about a year late.'

'I mean, after the christening, when you paid so much attention to my children and so little to the rest of us –'

He looked astonished. 'I'm sorry –'

'Oh for Pete's sake,' she burst out and rose to her feet. She crossed to the fireplace and put both hands on the mantelshelf. 'Are we talking or are we not? All right, I did stand you up about a year ago – not without reason, not without thought.'

He looked at her with considerable hostility. It showed through a cramped smile. 'I should have asked at once. D'you want some supper?' It was as if he were saying, 'You've violated my privacy, why not take some food as well?'

'You know I can't.' Had she not had to return to supper at home, a year before, the situation could have been different now. Dejectedly she sat down again.

'Ah,' he said in a forced way, suddenly taking a diary from his pocket, 'well, now, we'd better not forget your sons' education. You're right. We didn't have time on Saturday –'

Had he glanced up he would have seen the look of blank fury on her face.

'Didn't we really?' she asked not with satire, but in complete Glaswegian burlesque. 'Didn't we? Fancy that –'

But Sarson was not going to be drawn. Frowning at

8

his diary he turned over the pages, muttering, 'Education, Vass's brats – I made a note – in fact,' he went on,
'there's no special influence which can be used other
than an introduction to one of the young masters who
is forming a house list.' In the past years he had developed the heavy tones of someone whose authority is
never in doubt.

He still had not asked Stella to take off her coat, a
dark brown one which made her look like any modern
girl from the King's Road to Milan; the sort women buy
to unmarry themselves. She leant back in the chair now,
staring at him hard. But as soon as he started to lecture
again, she pitched forward to interrupt. 'I think I know
why I'm here.'

He paused for a second and looked up from his diary,
not directly at her but at the big oil-painted cows which
were held, in each painting, by men in tall hats with
short legs. More seriously, with lowered brow, he tried
again to guide her. 'I've met one or two of these young
men, and the master who looks after the house to which
my son will –'

She said, 'It's a highly moral reason.'

He closed his diary and put it back in his pocket. He
sighed, wearily. 'Oh dear, oh dear – I confess I'm surprised at you, Stella. Just because –' But then he hesitated.
He did not seem to want to recall their last meeting in
detail. He continued, vaguely, 'Just because the Marx
brothers stepped in on our last get-together, surely we
hardly need painful post-mortems a year later?'

'Who's in pain?' she asked, and a little blush appeared
along the line of his cheekbone as he recognised his own
arrogance.

9

'I'm an organised type,' she went on. 'That's really the trouble, I don't like loose ends.'

'I don't think I can be accused –'

'I know you can't. That's why I'm here. You can call it post-mortem or not, but the Marx brothers, as you so tenderly put it, had half my clothes off and me nearly on my back –'

'Oh really –' he muttered, rising to his feet.

'It's not them I'm blaming,' she added quickly. 'Nor questioning. I've enough confidence in this heap' – she indicated her whole body with a gesture of her wrist – 'to believe they had a fair enough motive. What has to be explained, in order to be forgiven, is why I bolted, next day. I think I'm too big for the feminine smelling-salts stuff, don't you? I don't like too much left unsaid.'

He sighed as if the conversation were an agony to him and soon she began to lose confidence in herself. She began to run on at such speed that she sounded as if she had no faith in what she was saying. It seemed to grow darker then and he did not switch on the lights. He stood looking out of the windows and she said, 'I asked you to be godfather as a kind of peace offer. I'm really saying sorry.' She lost her way for a moment, then grabbed at the point she had meant to build up to. 'The point is,' she said, 'in a young marriage, in a kind of children's marriage like ours – you know what Andrew is – well, it's not just adultery, then, it's iconoclasm too. When we took the vows, we meant every word of them, we –' She broke off again then said hopelessly, 'I didn't come here to say this at all. I don't know why I came here.'

He waited. She had stopped, but not because she had nothing left to say. It was all still there to be said. But she was suffering a sort of stage fright. It was as if the wind had blown straight off the pole, off Sarson, and caught her round the neck. She looked at him, pulled up the collar of her coat, then grabbed her handbag.

'As far as Andrew's concerned, I wasn't here, by the way,' she said and the choke in her voice now disappeared. Then she added, with something close to spite, 'I didn't come here with the idea of turning back any clocks, by the by. I'm not that stupid.'

He smiled quite warmly at her then, at this last moment, and said, 'You've got a talent for embarrassing scenes.'

'I'm glad I've got some talent.'

She tightened her belt. Realising, now, that she was preparing to leave, Sarson acted as if grievously disappointed. 'But where are you going?'

'I'm going.'

'But you haven't finished your drink. . . . You mustn't go as quickly as this. . . . Darling, that would be too unfair.'

'Oh God,' she said, with disgust at the conceit of all men, and she stepped over the end of the stool to get past him.

'No, please,' he said, catching her arm, 'I've been rude? I'm so sorry, my mind was on other things.'

'I don't believe you, Grandma.' She removed her arm and looked at him with dislike. Still looking him in the face, trying to search it, to find out whether he even thought he was telling the truth she then asked, 'Okay, what were you thinking about?'

'Somebody I saw in the street,' he answered truthfully.

'Who?'

He laughed. 'I don't think it'll mean much to you. In fact somebody who used to work for us. Now he's a representative of the International Monetary Fund. Are you any the wiser? I didn't know he was in London. It has its significance. . . . Now you'll stay –'

'Nothing would induce me to.'

He held his hands out, palms upwards.

'I've been rude again.'

She did not answer but made for the door. He stretched an arm and put his hand on the door handle, first.

'Please stay! No Marx brothers. I promise to be polite.'

Her eyes on her shoes, she replied, 'I'd rather just say, "Thank you, it's all forgotten."'

'But it isn't forgotten. Of course it isn't or why would you come here? For a clever girl, you do say some dotty things . . . why did you come here?'

'I don't know, I'm sure.' Then meekly, like the housemaid, she added, 'I can hear Salmon in the hall. Please may I go?'

He showed her out, with a pouting, sad expression on his face, but he came no farther than the flat door. He said, 'Looking like you do, you should never apologise,' and her anger rose up again. He said, 'I promise you, you're looking very well.'

'I know. Didn't you hear?' She was thinking back to the christening. 'I never look so common when I don't wear a hat.' And she walked swiftly away, biting her tongue, as he gave the same infuriatingly hearty laugh and closed the door.

Going down in the lift she was reminded suddenly, glaringly, of the scene that had preceded her descent almost a year before. She had blotted that from her mind for weeks now and she knew why. She had a talent for saying silly things to Sarson. She had left with a final promise to spend the following afternoon with him. She had been burnt by the sun that day. They had only called into the flat after a long day outside London.

'Man, banker, Sarson,' she had said, returning from the bathroom where she had been making up. The memory seemed now to cramp her. She held her shoulders an inch or two higher than usual in a strained way, as she recalled a terrible speech.

'Man, banker, Sarson, you with the arrogant pussy-cat face, one day, not today, this week, next week, some-time but not never, in a place unhaunted by bank, family or Salmon, I'll cup my hands around your neck, like this, only you won't be wearing a shirt. I shall follow down the line of your horrible upper-class neck, down your master-class sloping shoulders, until I finish grasping those big forearms with the blond yacht-owning fur on them.'

She had dropped on one knee, staring at him, still holding on to his sleeves. Then suddenly jumping up she had said, 'I think it's the shoulders. I think it's them.' Those were the last words, though she ran back to be kissed, before she got into this lift.

'Big tart you are, Stella,' she now thought.

The lift then stopped, and she recovered herself. But

it was not the ground floor. One of the concierges came in and said smoothly, 'Ground, madam?'

But at the bottom she did not get out. The concierge watched her curiously as she clanged the gate shut again. It was a very superior, gilded sort of lift.

He said, 'Anything wrong, miss?' and as she ascended, she replied, 'Can't I change my mind, son?' in a voice unlike any of the residents.

Salmon, at the flat door, looked quite panic-stricken, but before he could either announce her or refuse her she walked straight in. Sarson was still in the sitting room in which nobody ever sat. He was unpacking a parcel of books, neatly preserving the string.

'You've changed your mind,' he said with a pussy smile.

'I've done nothing of the kind.' She did not attempt to sit down but stood quite still only a few paces into the room. The door was not closed and Salmon hovered in the hall in the butler's traditional manner, out of sight, out of mind, but within earshot.

'You will eat?' Sarson asked, putting the little circle of string to one side and idly inspecting the new titles. She was controlling her breath only with difficulty. She looked much like a wartime girl, now; like one of our elder sisters with long straight hair and shoulders as square as a Wren's.

She sniffed, 'I won't be seeing you again until the next christening and I've got something to ask you.'

He put down the books and came quite close to her, fists on his hips. He was one of the few men who looked down on her and evidently he did so with pleasure. The cat's eyes were sparkling and half closed.

14

Determined not to be thrown by the smile, she went on quite firmly, 'Have you been bullying my husband this past month?'

He was hardly attending. 'Not that I know of. What makes you ask?'

'He's been a bit sad.'

'You *are* a pretty girl.'

'I'm asking seriously. I've got a hunch something's wrong.' She looked hard at him and he smiled and shook his head and very gently pushed his closed fist against her stomach.

'Not to my knowledge,' he said. He did not take the fist away.

'Would you tell me now if he has no future in Sarson's?'

Opening his hand, he said, 'Do push a little.'

'I asked you a fair enough question.'

'I can't remember what it was.'

'Are you thinking of sacking Andrew?'

'It's an impertinent question. But the answer is no, certainly not. Now you'll push.'

'No thank you, dear. Now I'll go away.'

'But you want to stay?'

'That's not the point. I knew I'd want to, but I'm not going to.'

'I suppose you're about the sexiest thing I've ever seen on two legs.'

'Forewarned, Sarson,' she said, slipping away, 'is fore-armed,' and he laughed.

He said, 'If you really think that, my darling, you've still got an awful lot to learn.'

'Oh, you big Tom —' she replied flatly as she left the room.

He had guessed she would go, so he did not protest. He just gave a little groan as she passed through the hall again, and said to Salmon, 'Supper for one, after all.'

You big tart, Stella. Oh, you big one, Stella Vass.

Chapter 2

As she retraced her steps along the thick red carpet back to Grosvenor Square, her ears should have been burning. Not that Sarson dwelt on her, after her departure; that would be impossible. A Sarson – so it's said, in the City – can safely be assumed to be thinking of one of four things: Sarson, the Sarson family, Sarsons Browne or Bradley on *Shakesperian Tragedy*. It was Andrew, Stella's pink-cheeked husband who was talking about her, at half past six, or thereabouts, in an upstairs room in the new Sarsons Browne office in Lombard Street.

The scene in the office, engineered by Andrew who had a kind of operatic talent for occasion, was out of date by sixty years. He had a bottle of champagne left over from the christening, on the previous Saturday, and he and his room-mate, Sarson's son-in-law, Alisdair, were drinking this by way of celebration. That morning, when he had smuggled the bottle in, the clerks and juniors, noticing the bulge under his coat, had said lots of things which made him feel superior. But in the event, the private party was very different from what the envious imagined. It did not, to begin with, celebrate the christening. And even Alisdair looked surprised when Andrew told him that.

'Mark you,' Andrew said, 'I don't see why we shouldn't wet the baby's head as well, but in fact the bottle celebrates a reprieve.' He nodded mysteriously. 'My reprieve.'

Paradoxes and even contradictions in terms seem to

be unavoidable in describing the Vasses, who married very young, and for this reason – so they said themselves – were as unlike as twin brother and sister. The present paradox was Andrew's phrenetic calm. Just as silence after a storm seems to have a special tension, Andrew, in this sad, thoughtful mood was not quite believable. The pink cheeks did not go with the curiously quiet, almost convalescent manner. Yet he did not seem to be putting on a pose. Usually, half way down the bottle he would be excitably drunk, indiscretions and inaccuracies not merely pouring but cascading out, one after the next.

'But not tonight,' he said. 'Not any more. I'm so tired of projecting more and more dangerous personalities in every bar in London that I'm prepared with great relief to sink back into a kind of grateful anonymity, breaking it only to write on lavatory walls from time to time, that Kilroy wasn't here. All my Kilroys have been exorcised. You don't believe it; neither, quite, do I. But I *hope* they've gone. I know as well as you do that only the weakest characters make strong new resolutions. Stella told me that on the first New Year's Eve we were married. But I'm grateful. I have reason to be grateful. Such reason that I sit here now in a kind of awe, exactly as if the death sentence had been removed from me. I need hardly add that it concerns Stella; and the children. This time last week I was absolutely sure I would lose both.'

Alisdair was the world's best listener. In protesting that he was quite out of his depths with Andrew he also flattered him. He said, 'I don't know whether I'm meant to guess, or not meant to ask questions, or what.'

18

'You're meant to enjoy the champagne.'

They sat opposite each other, both with their feet on their desks, which faced one another in a room shaped like a corridor. The last of the evening sun was streaming through the plate-glass window. Specks of dust shone in the shafts of light. The desks were modern, the chairs of light wood with blue-leather upholstery, as if made for a modern college; made to be photographed for the prospectus.

At last, Alisdair spoke again, holding his champagne in the shaft of light and rocking it in the office tumbler so that it looked almost viscous. As if thinking were very difficult for him, he said, 'I'm here if you want to volunteer information.' Then he continued, dreamily, 'Who doesn't enjoy confessions? The only thing better is confessing. I'm sure that's what gives gentlemen's clubs their special aura. Think what *hasn't* been confessed to in Boodles or Pratt's or one of those. . . . You know more about these things than me – I never get round to using my brain – but apart from the resolutions which we make in chapel every Sunday night and always break by Tuesday, isn't there a danger that you're being too tough on your former self? I mean, not to put too fine a point on it, don't blokes who love themselves too much in their twenties often make the worse mistake of hating themselves too much in their thirties . . . I don't know,' he added vaguely, taking a sip of champagne. 'I don't know. But I'm glad you're not going to lose Stella, if that's the final result. That's certainly worth a bottle.'

It was perfectly obvious that sooner or later Andrew was going to have to confess to the crime and to the meaning of the reprieve, and Alisdair said, 'Hurrah, at last,' very gently, when he got round to it.

'In spite of what you're thinking,' Andrew introduced the story wryly, 'it's not the greatest fun telling it. There's much more interest in the reprieve. The crime could hardly be more boring and squalid if it tried.'

'A typist in the family way?'

'No. But that level.'

'Adultery of sorts.'

'It goes farther and less far.'

Alisdair swung his feet to the ground. 'How fascinating,' he said. 'Is this why you've been so bouncy and cheerful and drunk and all that?'

'Exactly why, in here, and *molto piano* at home. But it's all over now.'

'Splendid,' Alisdair said. 'Please can I have more to drink?'

He had that special sort of modesty which made it possible for him to become totally involved in the speaker's argument or experience: a kind of superior gullibility.

'Come on,' he said now, 'we must have all the filthy details.'

'You can, in ten seconds: adultery intended, but not pulled off. Instead, trying to bring her to the point, I have a drunken supper, then go for a drive in what we called the country, which means in those roads with hedges between Egham and Staines, where sparrows fall.'

'I've got it,' Alisdair said, with certainty. 'You ran over a bobby.'

'Not a bobby, in fact,' Andrew replied smoothly, 'but

a middle-aged couple on their way to their firm's annual dance, and they were to receive some sort of presentation.'

'Not dead?'

'No, no. Not even much blood. But it was a head-on collision and they were bad enough to be whisked off to the Out-Patients' Department. . . . My bird then panics and cries and is sure her husband will find out. I do about the same but don't burst into tears. We make our statements to the police and the car, which I've hired for the outing, gets straightened out and we all creep home to await the dangerous and drunken driving charge which the policeman, who knows the other couple, more or less states will be made.'

'Were there other witnesses?'

'No. But I'm going well enough for a doctor to be brought in to examine me.'

Alisdair gave a groan. 'When on earth did it all happen?'

'That's the final cliché,' Andrew replied. 'Two months ago, when Stella was in hospital. Young husband celebrates birth of third son in usual, awful way.'

'You didn't tell Stella?'

'No,' Andrew replied. 'I'm a bit older than that.'

'Did you tell anybody?'

'Yes, of course. You know what the former Andrew was. Oddly enough I thought I was being stupid at the time; but that didn't stop me. I confessed to the nearest Daddy-figure, knowing that it is long past the time for me to have a Daddy-figure. Guess who.'

Alisdair said, 'I'm sitting here praying that it wasn't him.'

'Well it was.'

'And he said, in good J. T. Sarson tradition, "You've made an ass of yourself. If anything comes out you're sacked. Don't try and drag me in." Is that right?'

Andrew answered slowly. 'Quite wrong. Mark you, that's what I must have expected him to say. Fair enough. A bank's a bank. I suppose I drifted into his office in order not to prolong the agony. But then comes the surprise. He's more than helpful.'

'You told him about the other woman?'

'Yes.'

Alisdair nodded. 'That could appeal to the Boodles in his soul.'

Andrew shook his head. 'I suppose it did. But it doesn't sound enough to me. To tell you the truth, I still haven't an idea why he moved to the rescue. As you know, I can't think further than two stages – "If he says that, I'll do this" – so with Sarson, I just have to give up. Either he's five ahead, or else, extraordinary as it may seem, he likes me. Anyway, he did move to the rescue, in a super if faintly shocking way.'

'How?' Andrew could suddenly look thinner.

'I don't know how. But I'm not even going to tell you the result if you look stern like that.'

'I'm not sure I'm going to like it,' Alisdair admitted. His moral sense was always sharpest in discussing his father-in-law.

'You're not,' Andrew replied, 'but I trust you implicitly.'

'Boodles honour,' Alisdair said, but he was serious.

'He waved his wand. That's all I know. Whether his chum is the Lord Lieutenant or the High Sheriff or the

Chief Constable, I don't know. But on Friday evening I had to go down to the village where it all happened and there in a gloomy place like a schoolroom in a doll's house, some sort of deputy superintendent gave me a terrific dressing down, telling me he thought the police had evidence enough to take me to court and all that. I sat shivering as if it were mid-winter, until he said he had considered the background of the case, the birth of the baby, my clean licence and so on and then with a kind of highly suspect, beefy, good-sport smile he said the police were not going to press charges. So I shake hands and frankly grovel. Then, still a foot off the ground, I float back to the suburb, and we start in on the christening champagne.' Andrew looked up at his friend. 'You don't much like it, do you?'

'I'm glad for your sake,' Alisdair replied.

'But you're shocked and surprised.'

'Surprised only that he took the trouble.'

Alisdair smiled again. 'So now you're a reformed character.'

'The awful thing is,' Andrew replied, 'that I can't deny it. I really felt such a change in life at the week-end that it's a change *of* life. After the christening Stella seemed a bit down, so we went and spent a fortune staying at Claridges for the night, playing the sophisticated couple. But it didn't really hold up, in the bedroom. I just felt grateful, and holy and a little drunk. Usually we're good at playing rich maharajas and honeymoons.'

Alisdair didn't seem satisfied. He said, 'But didn't Stella notice something was wrong?'

'Of course she did. I told you, swagger hotels usually

do great things for us. . . . I think she put it down mainly to the morning drinks. But she gave me one or two piercing looks and asked me if we were in love.'

'And you answered you were.'

'Not directly. If I'd said it with the desperation that I felt I would have given everything away within five minutes. I answered her in Stella-language, saying, "We've acted in love for eight years, therefore we must be in love." . . . She liked that. Turned it over and over again in that head of hers, and was impressed. The evening cost about twenty pounds.'

Andrew had wandered to the window as he talked and peeped down at the deserted streets. But now he came back to his desk on which there were many papers with headings like this:

'THIS DOCUMENT IS IMPORTANT TO YOU, IF YOU DO NOT UNDERSTAND IT YOU SHOULD CONSULT YOUR STOCKBROKER OR BANK MANAGER WHO WILL EXPLAIN IT TO YOU. . . .'

They concerned a huge operation in which a German firm was buying a smaller Glasgow concern which manufactured turbine engines. He and Alisdair for three months now had lived under the shadow of 'Hamburg and Glasgow Turbines'. But they were in the last stages. The announcement that the offer was unconditional had now appeared in the Press. Neither of the two young men could possibly have guessed how important the last routine matters were going to be to them. On paper, all that had to be done was to convert the Deutschmarks

24

into sterling and make out cheques to the lucky Glasgow stockholders.

But they were in no mood to work now. Champagne and self analysis don't seem to make good companions. They had to laugh at themselves as they sadly finished the bottle and parted, stone-cold sober. But the warmth of the room, the curious, bright evening light and the empty bottle gave the whole scene a drowsiness. Breaking a long silence after they had tidied their papers away, Alisdair said, 'You see, you think about things, that's what's so wonderful. I never get round to thinking about things. Not really. I mean I can't have given Judas Iscariot a moment of my attention in seven years. I'm sure that's very bad. . . .'

Then typically he trimmed sail, and asked a closer question. 'If your former self, the Andrew we've known until now, the bouncy one – if he had been as awful as you rather suggest, then why did an intelligent girl like Stella stick with him?'

'I've thought about that. As far as I can make out he kept her love, if he kept her love, by the only known method. The one children use. He made constant demands on it: weeping, hollering, all fifty-six positions, all that.'

'Why did you say, "if he kept her love"?'

'I wouldn't dare not.'

'But she's no wind of your little drama?'

'None.'

'Then there's no reason to think she'll stop loving you.'

'Except that I've started to love her: not just to act as if I did. That's always scaring. I'll get jealous now and do all the wrong things for the right reasons.' He smiled as they parted. 'We all know how dangerous that is.'

The City was cool and clean and empty and frightening as Andrew wandered down the familiar lanes, into Copthall Avenue and through to Moorgate to catch a bus from there. He ran past the Wine House on the corner, past a passage where he had once seen an old stock-jobber weep at Christmastime, past the pub where the landlord literally died laughing at a bad joke. He walked past the door of number 20, the big building filled with stockbrokers' offices which inside looks like outside, like a gaol, with brick and stone stairs and little metal sidewalks leading to fire escapes. At rush-hour the office boys sprint out ahead of the clerks, while upstairs one of the brokers stays behind to do exercises with dumb-bells before returning home to a wife much tougher than himself. One of the clerks in the cashiers' department at Sarsons Browne, too, used to run home to Pinner with his suit in a brown-paper parcel carried under his arm.

It is as if the eccentrics, not the other hundred thousand, but the ones who weep and jump and run, who die laughing or topple from top-storey windows – as if all these, held in the mind in wildest detail, present the true picture; a kind of continuing individual disturbance that is corporate stability.

Walking between high buildings a city man has to hope that this fortress is his friend. Andrew did so with a prayer to no God and as if in answer, the half-hour was struck from churches and towers, from Mary-the-Axe to the Bells of Old Bailey.

26

Chapter 3

By eight o'clock in the suburbs, the only noises were the squeak of the chamois leathers polishing small saloon cars and the breezy 'Good-evening to you' of the publisher's representative who had succeeded again in selling some father a sixteen volume encyclopædia of which his children would tire in a week. Otherwise, silently, husbands were obliging wives who were not feeling at the top of their form, handing over to them the power and the responsibility which these same hatted ladies would later discover – by an unconsummated brief encounter, or, if they were the livelier sort, with a piercing scream in the night – that they never wanted in the first place.

Nowhere are feelings less strongly felt or a man's opinion less vigorously defended; nowhere therefore is life at a lower ebb than in the better suburbs of London – and the suburb in which Andrew and Stella lived could hardly have been more typical. It was called Temple Fortune, a nebulous area which is neither Golders Green nor yet Hampstead Garden Suburb, but boasts the worst characteristics of both. But the Vasses' neighbours (and also the rating authorities) insisted firmly that their house was in the Garden Suburb – sometimes, even in Hampstead, which was a good two miles away.

Number 313 describes their 'near-detached' house in a number. The garden was dull, small and sunless, the soil composed of London clay and London dirt. The high privet hedge made the back lawn seem even smaller

27

and the neighbours' dog had left more than fairy circles on the grass. The children's sandpit was filled with old plastic toys but there was no sand in it. The outside of the house was grey pebble and the windows and doors were in need of paint.

Within, the furniture did much to explain how the Vasses came to be living here. The house had been left to Andrew by a maiden aunt who had died shortly before he and Stella had fallen into each other's arms during a depressing vacational month at Oxford, when their 'real' friends were all away. No one had been more surprised than themselves when they bolted to Scotland and got married. But in fact, possession of the house probably gave Andrew the extra courage to elope, as he was considerably craftier than he liked to pretend, even in those days. He may have played his marriage as a reckless elopement, but it was safely underwritten by five thousand pounds' worth of brick, mortar and mahogany. A glance at the furniture made it clear that the maiden aunt had moved south from a large Victorian Scottish manse and had been loath to shed any of her belongings. Her scent lived after her. It was that curious smell which goes with ancient aunts and unearned income – especially if the income is small but the aunt big – not polish, not mothballs, not quite budgerigar, not lavender, not macassar, it was merely a damp and seedy aroma that had to be got used to, along with the mirrored sideboards, the patterned linoleum and the gloomy overhead lights.

Later that evening, questioning, grumbling, talking with her husband, Stella seemed to be at her happiest. She was in the same clothes, black stockings and brown skirt and pullover, but she had taken off her shoes.

'D'you know what it is, more than anything else, dearly beloved? I think it's that bloody bathroom, I do. That heater, or geyser or whatever it is that the torturing body who manufactured it likes to call it – it's too small, that's for certain. By the time I get in at night, I'm dead tired anyway. Maybe I've been in town like today and my arches aren't only flat, they're convex with those pavements. Soon I'm bawling and bickering at the boys and the two of them look so fragile and shivery, waiting for that wee drip of bath water, that I panic and I think "you bet, Stella, and tomorrow it's total war. So we'll all be strawberry jam." After that, ten to one, I catch the back of my nut on that linen-cupboard door that swings open and I'm sitting on the stool then, the mascara pouring down my cheeks. The boys don't look at me when I'm weeping, did you know that? . . . They're very snooty and suburban, our little boys, and that depresses me more. I suddenly see them grown men with bowler hats and clerk's wrists, coming back from the tube station at five past six, chatting to each other like love-birds. Sarson-slaves, exchanging inter-departmental jokes. . . . It's thoughts like that really stir the Jimmy Maxton – the old I.L.P. – in me and for some reason the only thing I can think of doing is blame you and all your works. And I see myself sitting astride you singing the Red Flag. And I'm sure that's dead psychosomatic. God knows what of. Of something – maybe life in Kelvingrove with the I.L.P. yelling at one end of the park and the couples in the bushes at the other. . . .'

Then running on in the same tone, with the same rapidity, her accent at its heaviest, she said, 'Can I confess something to you, my lawful wedded man?'

'It's never wise,' he said with a frown – and he looked very solemn and tired.

She put her hand out and touched the top of his head. She said, 'I believe you're getting adult and clerk-wristed and less erroneous and solecistic if that's what making howlers is, and not pink any more.'

They were in the kitchen, Andrew was on the table with his feet on one chair while she sat astride another, like a girl student.

He said, 'I'd never confess. I'm scared I'd lose you.'

She looked over her shoulder and said, with dread: 'Knock, knock?'

He was eating a piece of raw carrot he had found. But it was almost a fetish, this game. He was forced to reply, 'Who's there?'

'Therese,' spoken in a heavy highland accent.

'Therese who?'

'Therese the terrible pong in here, that pan must be burning for sure,' she replied, and suddenly rising, she hurried through to the gas cooker in the scullery and adjusted it. Then she came back, went up behind him and very firmly, with her big, broad white hand smoothed his brow. 'D'you mind I've got a loud voice? Answer.'

'I've got used to it.'

She pulled his head back. 'So you have. You're getting to keep your own trap shut, too, and I'm not sure that's such a good sign. I think you've been drinking to lower you to this degree of sobriety. Have you signed some pledge, dear heart. "Still waters" from here on?'

He smiled. 'No.'

'What's changed?'

'If I tell you, you'll only do me wrong.'

'It's time I did,' she answered cheerfully. 'Tell us.'

'I'm beginning to love you.'

Stella looked at him oddly. 'Is that why you won't let me make my grand confession? Are you scared the bubble would bust?'

'No. . . . The real truth is that I'd forgive you whatever you did.'

'Oh, don't say that. It sounds gloomy and resigned.'

'It's true.'

'I want to confess.'

He shrugged. 'If you want –' he said, going back to the carrots.

'Oh, that's not enthusiastic at all. You're not curious enough, d'you know that? That way you'll get old and wise and piles. You've got to squeeze confessions out of people, rave about the place, reduce the kids to tears – you should have seen my grandfather on an inquisition, slamming the doors and the women, all bones and balls and broth.'

'I told you,' he answered her, 'I don't want a confession that badly.'

'You don't want the truth in marriage?' she said, sitting down, as before.

'No. I don't need it.'

'That's very advanced, surely. . . . How d'you see us, with cigarette-holders and *double-entendres*, silk dressing gowns, ambiguities and ambivalences galore? Or hand in hand, Knight and Lady, Sir Dick and Lady Whittington enshrouded, forever and forgivingly, in a tissue of lies?'

He smiled and she sniffed and sighed and stood up. 'I'm famished,' she said. Then, with the ease of a Lido girl she raised one long, black-stockinged leg over the back of the chair and walked over to the dresser on which stood the one bottle in the house. It was a half bottle of brandy left over from the christening. She opened it, addressing him with her back towards him. 'I rang you this afternoon. I was feeling bad – but you must have been busy.'

'I was probably waiting for Hamburg. They kept my line clear most of the day.'

She had wandered next door again to deal with their supper, and she said vaguely, 'I'm a good Scotch cook which means to say if I don't get good Scotch beef and good Scotch vegetables to work with you get a lousy meal. I'm warming up to confess.'

Then, drying her hands on an apron that could have been cleaner, she stepped back into the kitchen. Andrew had not moved.

She said, 'I went out and looked at a cottage out off the Watford by-pass, behind the reservoir there. All the lot, it has: hollyhocks and thatched roof. I'm sure it's just like the one Nelson and that woman of his inhabited, if that's the word that covers it. Four bedrooms and another dreadful bathroom. It's bigger than it looks.'

'No,' Andrew said, with a slow shake of his head.

'I think we could knock them down in price.'

'I'm sure we could, but still "no". I'm sorry.'

'Why not?'

32

'Why did you go and look at it?'

She bit her lip, thought for a moment then replied, 'I've been bad this past month, rows and that, and honestly, I've tried with the women hereabouts, but I can't get anywhere. They just don't speak the same language. There's only one other girl been to school, and I'm not a snob that way, I mean Glasgow High's not exactly Cheltenham Ladies! Even if I did stagger into university, I've forgotten all I ever learnt. But she's not just forgotten, she's stuffed it right down, like an ugly secret as if having a degree might alter her peachy complexion; either that, or her vote. I lost my temper with her the other day. She wasn't awful pleased.'

She seemed to decide against telling the whole story. She began again.

'I bought her a bloody great bunch of flowers this morning, but she took them in with such a kind of starched "thank you", that I damned near shoved them in her face.'

Andrew sipped the brandy and water saying how foul it was, as she continued. 'I controlled myself, mind. I brought myself back, without assaulting anybody and I put myself on the couch next door, with the curtains half drawn and I said to myself, "Stella, dear child," you know, soothing-like – "Why is it, dear, that you are in a state of barely-suppressed violence? Would you not be better to go out and dig the garden?" Well, I knew I would, but I also knew I wasn't going to, so I slipped back to like I was when I was a little girl, convalescing, looking at the ceiling; I seemed to spend a lot of time like that. I must have been a ghastly, sickly child. That's how I read so well. . . . So then I stop feeling violent but begin to feel incredibly sexy, so I get up on my hind legs and say to myself, "This'll never do. Out of this, Stella Vass." Next thing I'm on a Green Line bus, and looking at a cottage for sale. I spoke to lots of people in the village there. I spoke nicely to them, about prams and village activities and the size of vicarages; I spoke calmly and sanely and nicely to them, as if I were a nice girl. They seem quite a unit, you know. A community, not just number 313, without a car. It's only four thousand, two hundred. I think we'd be happy there.'

'No,' he smiled quite kindly. 'It's just not on.'

'I don't think I can stand it here much longer.'

'You're not going to have to.'

But she ignored that note of hope. She had heard it before. She went on, 'Mind, I'm ashamed I can't. I sometimes think of poor Dame Henrietta Barnett with all her good intentions for the Garden Suburb and say to myself, "I'd like to have done that." There's nothing wrong with the idea at all. Except it just bloody well doesn't work and that's a fact. Couldn't we put a deposit down on this cottage?'

'We haven't got enough.'

'But if we sold this heap –'

'It's mortgaged.'

'We could get a mortgage out there. Would Sarsons lend you deposit money?'

'No.'

'Why shouldn't they?'

'That's not their business –'

'That's not the point. You're employed there. You work for them about ten hours a day, six days a week.'

He said, 'Darling, we're arguing stupidly. It's not the time to move yet. And actually it's not a time to ask the firm for money. In a few years we'll have much more money. . . .'

'To hell with "a few years",' she suddenly answered, no joke. 'To hell with that . . . why won't you look, sir? Andrew, what's got into you?'

He was surprised by her violence and answered coldly, as if he were hurt, 'I'm being perfectly realistic.'

'Realistic? That merit will be rewarded? That you too will have a big house in Sussex-by-the-City and your name on the notepaper?'

As her voice grew louder her face seemed to grow paler. Suddenly she was in a temper, her eyes hard and dark. He sat, for most of it, staring at his feet. She went on:

'Look, sir, look, look close. Look at Sarson's face, the cat that's swallowed the canary and do you know what that canary is? I'll tell you, seeing you're too loyal to open your eyes. It's nice new knowledge, like how to avoid deflation and slump and other things they've taught people like you; about inflation, full employment and that. And d'you know what the sum of it is? Instead of being run by a lot of ignorant, pirate-eating pirates your City's run now by pirates who don't even have that danger, and who get some smart advice. I'm telling you, all they do is just sit on top of the pile and smile their pussy smiles.'

Andrew was used to this sort of outburst. He answered, only, 'He doesn't smile at Alisdair. You should have seen him again today. Raving. I don't think he's forgiven him for marrying Elizabeth –'

'Don't you believe it. It's deeper than Oedipus, dear. It has to do with money.' She came closer and spoke urgently into his face. 'Of course he raves at Alisdair for whatever Alisdair does he's bound for the top of the pile and he should get in the habit of watching what he says. But you, dear? For Christ's sake, anyone can read it five miles off.'

He almost intoned: 'You're talking like a tub-thumper. You don't begin to know what Sarson's like, do you?' he said. 'He can be very kind.'

She seemed determined to make one last bid. 'Andrew, dear, see what you're doing. You're lying down like a lamb, you're resigning yourself to a place on the mat – if you call that being realistic.'

'On the contrary. I'm rowing in with Sarson.'

'You're rowing in, same as a press-ganged slave did, dear, under Captain Morgan. Of course you'll get more pay, like you would if you were selling soap. But that sort of increase doesn't make you richer, it just reminds you that you're getting on – the pun is all my own. And if things shift in the way all your other nice young Oxford assistants and managers say they will, then, sure, in the end your name will scrape on to the paper and, at current price, you'll buy one "A" share. One share, three votes, no power. . . . Andrew, it isn't the pay that counts. You know as well as I do. It'll go up and so will the tax. Your life's work will have got you into the place where you can run for Lord Mayor of London but all your snooty colleagues will think you pretty common if you do. Anyway, it'll only put you back ten thousand quid.'

She stopped and looked up. 'All better?' he asked. But she would not see it as a joke.

'I'm serious,' she said with a sniff. 'You're decadent, that's what you are. I think it's because you've got the sort of aunt who can leave you a horrible house. That saps a man, I'll bet – I'm grinning maybe, because I've got such a lovely wit I make myself laugh, but I'm serious underneath. It makes me red.'

'What, exactly?'

'Seeing Sarson sitting smiling on your smiling face. Can I put it clearer than that?'

He shook his head. That was all.

'Are you tired?' she asked.

'Yes.'

'Is that why you don't communicate?'

He put his hands on her shoulders. He said, 'I love you.'

'Most of all,' she replied, 'I hate and suspect you when you're all love and understanding. I suppose that's some sort of guilt. Andrew, why d'you stick with me?'

'Sex.'

'Is that true?'

'Basically.'

'I don't think it's like that with me.'

She saw the expression that passed across his face and laughed and put her hand on his leg. But tears rolled up in her eyes as she laughed. 'Oh, don't look like that, you silly, proud, vulnerable wee man. You're terrific at that. . . . But I don't think it's that which keeps me. I'm serious. I think I must love you.'

Then something strange and disturbing occurred. It was as if she looked at him too long and saw something in him which frightened her. A shadow seemed to flit across her own face, exactly as it might at the memory of a bad deed or tragedy. But she knew very well that this sorrow was not something from the past; it lay ahead. It was almost as if, for a second, Andrew's lashes had grown longer and softer. His was an expression both of anxiety and of love, almost of exhaustion, too; a sudden loss of momentum; a disturbing impression of a passivity which had little to do with the male.

Turning on her heel, Stella went back to the cooker in the scullery, but a moment later she had recovered herself. There was no hatred in her voice as she said, 'Isn't that an amazing thing? We must find each other fascinating. This bloody soup's boiled dry.'

Chapter 4

'Andrew?'

Any other husband would have said, 'Oh, no,' but Andrew answered, 'What is it, Love?' with the charity of a man newly snatched from the gallows. She woke him quite cheerfully at three in the morning.

'My brain's doing overtime,' she said. 'Perhaps I shouldn't have so many pillows.'

Outside there was silence. The lady in the upstairs room opposite and the nervous young mother of a new-born boy were the only other people awake in the suburb, the mother racked with anxiety, the old lady grown accustomed to pain.

'I told you a lie.'

'Oh, darling,' Andrew replied, 'of course you did. I told you, we're wrapped up in lies. So have I told you a hundred lies. Forget it, or better, stick to it, whatever it was.'

'In the game of the permanent ages,' she replied, 'you're one of the types that has two permanent ages. Sometimes you're twelve and sometimes like now you're a hundred and two.' Then she added, more generally, 'Mind it doesn't make it easy for me, because each time I think of laying my head safely to rest in the lap of the man that's a hundred and two, the twelve year old slaps my face.'

'I've given up being twelve,' he replied, but she did not bother to tell him how often that had happened before.

She was confessing again. 'I didn't go to the cottage off the Watford by-pass this afternoon. I went about a week ago.'

'That's not so important.'

'Oh, but it is,' she said. 'Today I went to meet a man.'

He stirred. 'In Hyde Park,' he suggested, 'by the Serpentine.'

She paused a moment, then she answered, and at once started counting out loud. 'Nope. In a flat in Grosvenor Square, one, two, three, four, five –'

'Sarson?'

'Right you are,' she replied, 'and double your money. Do you want to ask me another?'

'Why did you see him?'

Stella clicked her teeth. She said, 'You disappoint me, really you do. You should leap to the wrong conclusion.'

He answered, 'I thought anything that was going to happen would have happened a year ago, the day he took you out to that Adult Education Place.'

'You clever man,' she said, 'that's absolutely right.'

'Then why did you go and see him?'

'You still disappoint me, dear heart,' she replied, then began to explain. 'Really you do, asking a "why".'

'I'm interested in the answer.'

'Interested?' She said loudly, 'I'm absolutely fascinated, but use your loaf, dear, you don't just ask why. That way you get back a load of lies, for sure, some intended, some conscious, some subconscious, some purely by the way, thanks to the deficiencies of definition, language, all the rest of it. Did you never go to those lectures?'

He answered steadily, at a hundred and two, 'If you

really want to tell me about it, do so. Just pretend I'm not here and spout. . . . Have you something to hide?'

'Of course I've something to hide,' she said, almost huffily.

'What?'

'Oh, Andrew, please, come on. . . . "What"? Of course I don't know. If I did know my brain wouldn't be whizzing around in circles at three in the morning, would it?'

'It's a kind of Red Queen logic, you have.'

'I am the Red Queen,' she replied strongly. Then she said, 'It's quite warm. D'you think I'd be better telling this confession – *mea maxima culpa* – with my nightie off? I think I would,' she answered herself and at once with a great struggle pulled her black nightdress over her head and flung it on to the floor. If Andrew had not slept in the same bedroom nothing would ever have been hung up. She sat up against the pillows so that her breasts lay above the sheet; splendidly shaped, deep, with huge nipples.

'The way to answer "why" is to ignore it, I'm sure about that. I'll tell you what happened, you work out why.'

She waited and he said nothing. Then in exactly the same tone she said, 'I'll tell you what happened, you work out why.'

Still he did not move. This time, levelly, but at a level a fraction higher in pitch, she said yet again, 'I'll tell you what happened, you work out why,' and he stretched his hand across and touched her, not with fingertips, but warmly with the whole palm of his hand.

41

She said, 'I'm trying to tell you that I love you,' and she was crying. She said, 'I hate my easy tears.'

He turned round and smiled at her, 'No comments, no statements. Your rules.'

'Right,' she said and sat up a little straighter. Then at last, she began.

'Scene One, Stella looking very with it, King's Road type, only more weight, there I am, dig me daddy, walking across Grosvenor Square giving hang-dog late afternoon business men and club members sharp brush-off as they take in the black stockings.'

'We're interested in what's going on inside your head,' Andrew reminded her and she answered, swiftly:

'I know. I know that, dear heart, but you've got to stalk it. Mostly I'm an actress, thinking about herself crossing Grosvenor Square, in one of these freeze moods when one is acting just ahead of self-knowledge. Maybe I'm not making myself clear but it's important, this bit. I know that, because it makes me a little breathless telling it, and at the time, as I glanced at one of these bods with the sandwich boards saying "No Nuclear Tests" I got a bout of the old asthma, so something was going on. Anyway I persevered – so into the flats I go.'

'How d'you know where?'

'I've been there when we came back from Adult Education and all that, a year ago. I think you picked us up there.'

'I didn't.'

'No, I remember now. Cousin George took me home. He came and collected me in a pub round the corner, but we're talking about today.'

'I just thought the two visits might be connected.'

'Maybe, but not the way you're thinking, which I can tell in your voice.'

'I didn't mean sex.'

'And I didn't say there wasn't sex in it. I told you, I'd quite a bad spot of breathlessness for some reason and I hadn't any dope with me. So I sit down just inside the flats.'

'Smell?'

'Good for you. It's questions like that make me think we'll always live together . . . smell? Let me see, or let me sniff. Sense of smell wasn't too strong about then, as you'd guess. I was sitting on a kind of black piano stool, my feet half on the marble, half on the thick red carpet – got it? The carpet must have been new. There's carpet, pile carpet smell, not that my nose is very keen, and there's also a kind of coolness, and noises off like noises in a ship. The lift is painted black and gold. At last I recover myself, and checking his number on the Board, Mr and Mrs J. T. Sarson, I go up to floor number four and get out where there's no daylight, blinking like a bat. Somebody presses the lift which vanishes and leaves a big hole behind me.'

'Inside the head?'

'Inside –' she repeated, trying hard, scowling. Then she let go with, ' "This is a dare, Stella MacNaughten" – because I'm not Stella Vass at that moment, any more – "This is a dare and if you funk it this time, I'll just dare you again." . . . That's as near as I can get it.' She paused. Something closer to the truth seemed to pass through her head and disturb her, disturb the whole air round about her.

43

Andrew prompted, 'You rang the bell and somebody comes to the door –'

'No, wait,' she said suddenly, 'it's ridiculous going right through. I think I've got the answer; wait, wait . . . it's on the tip of my tongue.'

'Ad lib,' he suggested.

'Right, ad lib, coming up. When I'm inside I'm on the grovel a bit, I'm saying to him we're highly honoured he agreed to be godfather – the honour is ours –' She paused. Her mind was not completely on what she was saying. She spoke dreamily, 'And then I bring forth my excuse for being there and say, "What about the boys' education?" – Mind, then, I thought it was my real motive, the reason behind the trip, but I see it now – the reason's in the grovelling. . . . I'm fairly steamed up about this education, admitting, ha-ha-ha, I'm a socialist myself but in a capitalist society, "Do what the capitalists do and enjoy it if you can". . . .' Again she frowned as if this synthesis of a scene, this lie for a scene, had exposed something too close to the truth. 'And I'm going on about you, covering up, saying if you knew I was troubling him for the necessary introduction you'd be wild, so please, please on his honour, would be keep his mouth shut. . . . In a way too, I'm behaving like you at your worst, flashing the smooth skin and the baby fat telling how I've come up in the world, maybe – at least, so all my relations back in Glasgow think; I went on about my father being the reader at the works after being on the machines, composing almost fault-lessly for nearly fifteen years. The detail' – she broke off with – 'the detail, the ends to which we go.' And the comment then was more than ambiguous. Within the

44

remark was a clue to the whole labyrinth of lies. 'The detail' referred first to the ends she was going to, to lie to Andrew; but second, the meaning, as stated, was her surprise at the details which she told Sarson, because she had told him all these things and at a time when she did not believe that she was grovelling to him, namely a year before, when he had taken her out to this College of Adult Education.

She was lost for a moment, silent in her own thoughts. Was displacement in time, like that, really a lie? He did not prompt her now, and at last she said, 'Are you asleep or just pretending to be?' They seemed to have floated apart.

'Neither. I'm waiting.'

'You're good at waiting. Too good at waiting, maybe. Perhaps that's wrong. Perhaps you should knock me over and rape me like they do in Australian plays. Anyway, the silence has brought forth an answer to "why".' She sounded altogether more desperate, now; as if hating herself. 'A disgusting, horrible answer which explains why it wasn't so easy to grasp and also why I was going at you so vehemently downstairs to-night for doing absolutely the right thing, just sticking to your job on the lap that really matters . . . I am duly eating humble pie. I went to Sarson because I was afraid. Seeing him again at the christening made me think of that other occasion last year, when I don't say he wanted to rape me literally – I shouldn't think he touches girls my class, either above or below – the class I mean, not the position –' Then she stopped, as the sentence over-whelmed her. She tied it all up, at last, by starting again. 'I saw him at the christening. I remembered I'd refused

45

this job he wanted to give me at the Adult Education dump. I'd refused because I was scared of getting under his fatal spell, because at that time you were a bit in love with him which annoyed me, I suppose. Now today, remembering I'd refused him, I grew more scared and so I went back, like the housemaid, to suck up.'

'It's an answer,' he agreed. 'But you didn't need to, you know. He thinks a great deal of you. He told me once. Actually when you went into hospital, this time, he gave me a drink in the Athenaeum.'

'That was big of him. Was it a double?'

'It was very civil. Let's leave it at that. But he likes you.'

'That's nice to know.'

'You shouldn't be so chippy.'

'You won't tell him I told you about the visit?'

'Of course not.'

'I don't know why I ask you that –' she said, amazed how some lies sound, indeed seem to be truer than the truth. 'But for some reason I wouldn't like him to know. Maybe it looks like a double-grovel. . . . You should have been born one class lower, dear, then you'd get bigger kicks. It's not really in you to hate the English gentleman, but I can assure you he's a very satisfying object for hatred.'

But Andrew was tiring. He touched her, then rolled over.

She smiled then, and clicked her teeth. 'We just don't use our brains enough. We're slow.' She looked down at her breasts. 'Look at me, making a clean breast of it, and we never noticed that. You liar, Stella. Oh, you big one, Stella Vass.'

46

She brought the bed-clothes up to her neck but still did not think of sleeping. Looking at the reflections on the ceiling she remembered then, exactly, how she had twisted her own arm in order to make herself ring the bell of Sarson's flat.

She had simply said to herself, 'If I've gone to the trouble of coming this far, then I'm serious, whatever my reasons. And if I'm serious and don't go in this time, then I know what the pattern will be. It will happen again and again. So I might as well jump now.'

Then she thought, 'And I didn't jump,' but her mind would not go forward from there.

As if to escape from her own thoughts she spoke out loud again. 'You're too good to be true, tonight, tender heart. Are you contemplating murdering me?'

'Macbeth has murdered sleep,' he replied drowsily, but she would not take the hint. She continued:

'You should be very strict with me, not all understanding. That never leads the right way. What about that business on Saturday night? You're tired so I haul you out to Claridges: caviar, all that. I didn't need all that.'

But he did not reply.

Soon, outside, there was a shower of rain. It fell hard against the leaves and the smell of it seeped in. Stella's hands were stretched towards the ceiling. They shone in the light of the street lamp, as she clasped and unclasped them. The shadows of the branches of a weak little birch tree by the street lamp waved about like the reflection of water, on the ceiling. She said, 'Whatever money I had, I'd spend too much.'

47

But if he were still awake he did not encourage her with an answer.

'Money's downright evil, so it is. I know they teach you that when you're a kid and it sounded simple-minded to say it, but it's right. Money's nothing to do with happiness I'm sure, any more than a sunken bath has to do with love. It's something evil in us makes us join the two. Money would spoil what we have. Money wouldn't just age us. It's like that apple. One bite and we'd be old.'

Then one of her sons, next door, stirred in his sleep. It was Josh, the three-year-old. She sat up at once. It was quite unnecessary for her to go to him but she seemed to want to. She put on a woollen dressing-gown and went through to sit by his bedside, in the cold. Outside the rain had stopped. Very gently she swept the hair from his brow.

A quarter of an hour later she returned to her room and Andrew was again asleep, his lashes long and soft and dark against his cheek. Climbing into bed heavily as if purposely trying to wake him, she said of her children, 'Mice! That's what they are. I sometimes get in a panic thinking the bomb'll do for all of us, but leave the mice behind.'

Then, still brightly, she said, 'What will actually happen when the bomb drops is that Josh will nod twice, where we are, in our shelter, then ask me, "Mummy, was that a big one? Was that a really big one?"' She laughed softly and congratulated herself. 'That's Josh, exactly.'

Chapter 5

As Andrew seemed incapable of distinguishing between positive virtue and a moral hangover, life for a few days remained suspended in an atmosphere which Stella described distastefully but aptly as loving glumness. Then suddenly it changed dramatically. Stella at once reacted to Andrew's vitality when he returned on the Friday evening, bubbling over with excitement. He started telling her the news downstairs, and delighted by him, reassured in the nick of time, she grabbed his arm very tightly and led him, still talking, upstairs to the bathroom where first she bathed the boys.

But a little honesty is a dangerous thing. Telling three-quarters of the story, Andrew put his head straight into a noose. At the beginning there was no indication of the trouble that lay ahead. Quick to notice Stella's delight at the change of mood, his description became more vivid, and slanderous, every moment. He seemed to be telling the tale at this stage only because it was bursting out of him.

'Salmon and salad and hock, thank you,' he described a meeting of the Directors of the Bank of England in the language which was private to Alisdair, Stella and himself. She replied, as if providing the second couplet of the chorus:

'Who's for a point off the Bank Rate? . . . . Two dozen roses to the matron.'

Nobody in Sarsons Browne, other than J. T. Sarson who was a director of the central bank, had any clear idea of what happened at these luncheons in Threadneedle Street, for the simple reason that no outsiders attend the Governor's Court. But details have leaked out. Cold salmon, in season, is a popular lunch. The flowers are often sent to the matron of one of the London hospitals, with the Governor's compliments, later in the afternoon. The wines are known. And Andrew had often seen the gentlemen returning to their separate banks, all except the permanent servants who remain in Threadneedle Street. Like statesmen or generals, they tend to have their idiosyncrasies: the silver hair in the wind; or the bowler tipped back in what Andrew now described as the early Tory manner, F. E. Smithish – the angle of appealing arrogance.

'. . . Sarson, of course, our man in Threadneedle Street, the least dressy, the biggest ram, has Lockhart's *Life of Scott* tucked under his arm, I expect. Anyway the point is that they broke up earlier than usual today and this threw Alisdair and me, who hadn't checked all the chits that had to go to him after lunch.'

'Facts?' she asked.

'Very important facts. The two chits wind up the Glasgow Turbine thing. They're merely instructions signed by Sarson, one to the head cashier, the other to Foreign Department. The first says "Sign, check and despatch the Glasgow shareholders' money", the other says "Instruct the joint-stock people to exchange the Hamburg Deutschmarks into pounds sterling at once, this afternoon, and credit to our account as cheques to that value are being despatched to the Glasgow stockholders this afternoon."'

Stella was bathing the boys as she listened. She told

them to shut up when they tried to interrupt and she urged Andrew to continue. 'Come on, dear heart, I can tell you've swallowed a swan. Let's have it all.'

'Right,' Andrew said. 'Telephones ring, signals go up and Miss Parker wafts up and down in the lift saying "J.T.'s in" as if Mafeking's been relieved – all beads and bottom, our Miss Parker, especially when she's one up on Alisdair and me. As fast as we can go we gather all the papers, cheques and the two instruction notes together, do up our waistcoat buttons, and as bright as fags, hurry downstairs, expecting to find him champing at the bit. But no. Surprise, surprise. We find him in his light overcoat, which only he would wear on a day like this, playing vaguely, unseriously at cricket strokes with his rolled umbrella. While he does this, a big pussy smile all over his pussy face, we stand about more and more like sycophantic schoolboys, only Alisdair modifies his admiration with a rather half-hearted frown.'

'C'mon, C'mon,' Stella said, sailing boats up and down the bath, to keep the children quiet. 'What's he saying?'

'He's saying,' Andrew replied, 'the most extraordinary things and I'm not going to give you any hints. I twigged fairly soon, rather surprising myself; certainly sooner than Alisdair. But you've got to guess. This is a house-party quiz for boys waiting to get into Merchant Banking. First he's saying things like, "I never was any good at cricket." And nodding at Alisdair, saying, "We're leaving it to Alisdair there to repair the family's athletic reputation." He's going on like this, saying his son Paul's a wash-out at cricket, and does it run in families? Alisdair, slightly curtly, because he hates being reminded

51

in the office that he's a games player, is providing inadequate answers.'

They were interrupted for a moment by the screams as the boys were hauled from their bath. Then Andrew asked, 'House-party question number one, how does the boy manager react?'

Stella thought quite seriously. She said, 'Whatever the boy manager may be thinking, he reacts the same, with the old Jeeves treatment. "If the chairman decides he wants to talk about his own athletic inadequacies, who am I to object?"'

'Right,' Andrew said. 'At least I think "right", and as Alisdair pulls up a chair and slightly officiously plonks all the papers on the end of the desk, Sarson takes absolutely no notice of him, and about here my brain, surprisingly enough, begins to tick. Sarson smoothly pushes the papers to one side, and leans his backside against the desk. He is holding his umbrella upside down swinging it lightly, held firmly between huge fingers and thumb. It goes to and fro like a pendulum, making me wonder just for a second if there's been more hock consumed than cold salmon. But he's sober enough, and now very lazily he changes his tack.

'"Honestly," Sarson talking, "I've enough worries without you two harrying me." He puts the brolly down like a sword on the table and shoves his hair back from his forehead – all very boyish stuff. I can't give you it verbatim for the simple reason that it went on and on and on. Quite funny really, all about his domestic arrangements, each morning. How breakfast is spent in the Sarson household arguing about who'll go where in each car. "Salmon will take Jennifer up to Knightsbridge, then run Caroline over to meet her chums at the Zoo. He'll drop the Mini for servicing at the garage by the station, then Jennifer can pick it up if she comes back by the five o'clock express. Salmon can pick up the children, return by the City at five, drop them all at Grosvenor Square for a cup of tea, then when Alisdair and Elizabeth turn up they'll all go down to the country together – except somebody must pick up the German girl whom cousin Tom is leaving, to be called for, at Harrods. . . ." He goes on and on like this. All very convincing. I've heard him myself talking like this for hours on the 'phone. What he calls "the infinite commutations of two cars, one house, one flat, one wife, two daughters, a son-in-law and a son", not mentioning the three really complicating factors of a steady mistress, the girl he means to make next week, and a fortune in the bank.'

Stella said, quickly, 'About how long does this go on?'

'It seemed an age, but truly for seven or eight minutes, without a break.'

'A kind of filibuster?' Stella asked and Andrew smiled.

He said, 'It's absolutely ruinous to be married to an intelligent girl. I do wish I had a wife who would never grasp the point and have to have things explained in one syllable, slowly.'

Stella sniffed; stopped drying her sons for a moment. They were wrapped in huge towels. Then starting to dry the little one, Josh, again, she said, 'Continue with the facts, I'm not quite sure I have got the point. Give us all the data.'

53

'Very well. At last he dries up, and he looks rather dyspeptic for a moment and swallows an indigestion pill. I sort of stand at the ready, but I don't grab a chair and I don't fumble with any papers. Alisdair, meantime, rather purposefully, I thought, but perhaps just to show his own efficiency, says, "We've got the cheques. That's the last item on the programme," and Sarson looks more and more displeased. For a second, but not with the same good humour, indeed almost bitterly, he returned to arrangements. With a sigh he said, "The long and the short of this morning's two hours' discussion of itineraries is that I have to go down to the country by train."' Andrew stopped. Stella was all eyes. Andrew said, 'Ace question, girl graduate? What does the manager do?'

Stella was about to answer, then she seemed to decide against it. Only the girl at the top of the class can swallow the right answer. 'You tell me.'

'But you –'

'Come on, you're being infuriating. Tell me what you did?'

Andrew said, with a complacent smile, 'Soft but swiftly on the cue, I said, "It's Friday, sir, unless you catch one of the earlier trains you probably won't get a seat." The clouds lift. I have definitely given the right answer. He sits down, stretches out his legs and as lazily as a Lloyds man, he drawls, "That *is* kind of you, Andrew, I must say I'm rather weary."'

'Then?'

'Well then, Alisdair grew rather obstinate for a second, shoving the chits forward saying, "There are only a couple of things to sign," but I know I'm right

54

by now because he absolutely ignores Alisdair. . . .
Actually, I was rather shocked by Alisdair because he
kept pressing tactlessly, but anyway it's arranged between Sarson and me that the programme is adjusted –
the Marks to be paid out on Monday, cheques then too.
. . . But not today.' He looked at her, still proud of
himself, and said, 'I wonder if you do get the point?'

'I'm not sure,' she replied, then called Elsa, the
German girl, to take the children to the bedroom and
put their pyjamas on. Not three minutes later, however, they came back, fascinated by talk which they
could not understand.

Stella seemed to be making up her mind. She looked
quite grave but she spoke as wildly as ever. It was as if
the wheels inside her, huge heavy cogs and main fly-
wheel were rolling slowly into action. By then she had
decided to give herself a bath, and to the boys' excitement she went downstairs and returned with two huge
kettles of scalding hot water.

'In my nakedness and as an obsessional talker out-
talked,' she said, looking at her sons, 'I should like to
announce to you gentlemen that some of the most
eminent members of the English Bar and Bench believe
it's thoroughly wicked, disgusting and immoral that
young boys should see these things which previously
only the butler saw – such as me,' she added, leaping
out of the bath again, 'getting my toes burnt.'

Andrew knew her too well to hurry her. She would
return to the question in her own good time.

David, the elder boy, said, 'Do you think the Queen
will answer me, if I write to her?' and she seemed
happy to cope first with his problem.

'I'm not sure about that.'

Andrew warned his son, cheerfully, 'She has a lot of letters to answer already.'

'But she might answer me.'

Stella explained. 'It's that Elsa,' she said. 'She's got a thing about royalty. It's our big Prussian bumble bee.'

'She's got a book about the Queen,' David said, while his young brother threw the boat back into the bath. 'Does the Queen have a shelter in her garden?'

'I'm sure she does,' Stella said. Then, as she settled down in the bath she bit her nail and said vaguely, 'I don't know whether this is wonderful or terrible, what my husband has been telling me, but I'm sure it's important. If all your guesses are right and we devalued ten per cent over the week-end just for instance, how much would Sarsons stand to gain?'

'In sterling?' Andrew thought for a moment. 'There's a lot of money involved. Ten per cent would mean a gain of about £400,000.' He did not bother to congratulate her for getting there in one.

Stella grabbed the huge tablet of bath soap, which she kept hidden behind the monstrous geyser. She said, 'It's very good really,' still in the same wary, purring tone, as if underneath the calm surface of her mind was now revved up to Full Speed Ahead. 'It's as easy a way of increasing a margin as ever I saw. . . .'

And Andrew, innocently, nodded in agreement. She saw that, but did not comment.

Josh leant over the side of the bath and knocked his boat against her leg, persistently and harder each time until she said she would hit him if he did it again. David meantime had fetched The Book. Andrew sat down on the closed lavatory seat and smoked a cigarette.

Stella was still nosing round the subject, apparently uncertain of her exact standpoint. She said, 'It's a moral conundrum, all right, all right. I'm torn in two still, the prudent mother versus Miss Jimmy Maxton. Do you realise that?'

Andrew said, 'I don't think it's our problem either way: but I think I'm right about what's happening.'

Stella looked round the tiny crowded room from the underclothes piled on the floor to the steam curling along the ceiling. She ignored his remark. 'The thing about Communist living,' she said, 'is that it must be just like this. I once saw a film about Warsaw. It's the inconvenience, isn't it, that makes it so attractive? I think the Americans ought to go easy on the children's bathrooms and that stuff. Maybe they haven't thought it out deep enough. I'm not sure at all, that we want all that comfort.'

'What sort of dog is that?' David asked, jamming the book in front of his father.

'A corgi,' Andrew said.

The steam seemed to clear. Stella said the water was right for the first time in three months and Andrew began to take off his tie and coat.

Stella said, 'I think I understand what's happening.'

'Of course you do' – Andrew replied, but before he could continue she interrupted in a voice which was as obvious a warning as a siren with an undulating note.

'Dear heart, the only thing that makes me wonder if I don't understand is your attitude.'

57

'What d'you mean, "my attitude"?' He sounded genuinely puzzled.

'Let's take it slowly; let's have no misunderstandings,' she replied. 'I'll go one by one, step by step, like the wife you really want –' There was a hard edge to the remark.

'You know I didn't mean that –' he protested.

'Be that as it may,' she said, again wailing out a warning. 'I'd hate there to be misunderstandings. Let's get it all straight and clear. Our life,' she added vaguely, 'maybe depends on it.'

The warning had small effect. The only reaction from Andrew was a shrug and one covering remark. He said, 'Either way it's your opinion or my opinion. There aren't any hard facts –'

'There seem enough facts for me. One, you've got a programme for this take-over thing, this Hamburg-Glasgow. Can I ask you some questions?' She glanced up and added in the same breath, 'Dear heart, I'm going to ask some questions.'

Slowly he began to undress.

She said, 'Unless Sarson was very ill or had some ulterior motive we would expect the Marks to be converted and cheques to be paid out today, Friday, as per programme. Am I right?'

'Yes.'

'And Sarson isn't very ill.'

'He said he was tired.'

She lay back in the water and muttered that it was all too obvious what was happening. Andrew seemed determined to be cheerful. It is an ill wind that blows no good.

Saying so, he sounded like a prospective candidate at a tea party.

He confided, 'For a little while last month – you may have noticed – I thought I was in a bit of trouble.'

Certainly she had noticed. 'What sort of trouble?'

'Oh, office trouble – only that. I mean I thought I was a bit out of favour with Sarson. That's why I've been a bit quiet. But this is a good day. Please don't get all worked up about it and discuss principles and that, Stella. I can see that's what you're liable to do. But it's not real to do so. It's Kelvingrove hangover, that. The real thing is that I shouldn't lose a job, shouldn't even be out of favour; the real thing is us here.' He indicated the children. He said, 'Anything else is just getting political and false, it's like people who say mental torture is worse than a red-hot poker in the eye.'

He was leaning forward, talking urgently to her but she would not look up at him. He went on, 'Anyway, we could be quite wrong. There probably won't be any devaluation. We're maybe adding two and two to make five. Let's not have one of those awful political engagement rows,' and he looked at her where she lay, naked in the bath. He smiled, and made a face behind the children's back. He said, with complete sexual confidence, 'We've got much better things to do.'

She soaped her ankles and first answered her son dreamily, 'Yes, dear, at Windsor,' when he asked if the Queen still had corgis.

'Who looks after them?'

'The Master of Corgis,' she answered at once, then sent both children out, because Elsa was ready to put them to bed. When they'd gone she said, 'You've got to face it, the corgi and that has a strong educational value. That's the only book he's ever been interested in – really sold on, you know? Can you tell me why?'

Andrew shook his head, threw his cigarette out of the window and hung up his suit on the back of the door, which for some unfathomable reason was covered with a shiny 'imitation wood' wallpaper. He took a big towel from the linen cupboard and she stepped out of the bath and sat on the edge, enveloped in it. He climbed in, lay back and began to play with the boat.

Stella said, 'I'm coming slowly to some conclusions and I'm not sure you're going to like them.'

'Oh, Stella –'

'Am I right, it starts with the meeting of the Court in Threadneedle Street?'

'No,' he interrupted, lying back again. He said quite openly, 'Now I come to think of it, it starts before that.'

'Let's have it all.'

Andrew nodded. 'It starts in fact, last week, sometime, with a cabaret, in Sarson's room.'

'What about?'

'About the last items on the Hamburg-Glasgow programme. We still had to convert the Marks and pay out the cheques. Sarson decided to turn it into one of his nastier tutorials and instead of instructing me to do this according to the programme, conversion Tuesday for pay-out Friday, he decided to put questions to Alisdair.'

'Such as, "When do we pay out, Alisdair?"'

'Exactly. And Alisdair as usual froze up. It went on for about ten gruesome minutes before Alisdair at last came round to saying that if the reserves were low, as per chancellor's statement, last week, and therefore, the pound soft, it would be wiser to hold the cash in Marks until the last moment.'

'But he said it in the end?'

'Yes.'

'And Sarson?'

'I'm just remembering. He did look rather satisfied I think, as if something which he didn't want to say himself had still been firmly said.' Andrew nodded, shifted up the bath and said, 'Yes. That's really when it started.'

'You didn't say anything to me about it.'

'I didn't snap, I suppose.'

'But didn't Alisdair and you just wonder a little about a director of the Bank of England guiding his son-in-law into saying there might be devaluation? Was there no tiny bell ringing at the back of your heads?'

'If there was, we didn't discuss it.'

'Oh, Andrew, I thought you were bosom friends –' She spoke roughly, impatiently, and Andrew's reserve began to return. He shrugged like a scolded child.

'It's always awkward when one of the partners is also in Threadneedle Street. As much as possible one avoids this sort of discussion. After all Sarson's half a public servant. One can't make it awkward for him. It's like asking the King's valet if the old man wears a Y front.'

'Andrew, it must have gone through your brain.'

'It didn't stick there,' he replied obstinately, 'or I would have told you that evening. Perhaps I wasn't bright enough to add two and two.'

She kept drying herself for a moment, then he spoke

61

again. 'What I think happened was that I dismissed the idea as altogether too obvious. If there was going to be devaluation then Sarson would be bound to avoid any discussion in that whole area.'

She looked at him solemnly. 'It does seem a bit on the nose,' she admitted. 'But didn't Alisdair say *anything*?'

Andrew stirred. 'As I remember he raved about our room flinging circulars in the waste-paper basket saying, "It's so bloody easy for him." He often goes into little hymns of hate, starting with Sarson, ending always with himself. "The trouble with me," he says, usually, "is that I don't despise myself with sufficient intensity." So instead of leaving or answering Sarson back, he just toddles home each evening to his fantastically beautiful wife, pours himself a scotch-on-the-rocks, thinks about golf and sinks into the chintzes. He often asks me if I hate and despise him.'

'But you love him.'

'He's my best chum, let's say.'

Stella stared at him for a moment. Then she said, 'There must be an indolent streak in you somewhere in spite of all the bubbles and glands. D'you know you never soap yourself in the bath? You never wash at all.'

Then, as he lay there smiling, she took him quickly by surprise. 'Sarson didn't pay you off?'

'No. What on earth makes you think that?'

'Not necessarily with money –'

'He didn't pay me off.'

She looked at him still as if she did not believe him, then she switched the subject back. 'There's one thing that worries me. Won't the German gentlemen object?'

'They've got no grounds.'

'What d'you mean, they've got no grounds? They paid out three million or thereabouts in Marks: you convert and only have to pay out, say, ninety per cent of that. Surely one of them stops and says, "Hey, we paid out a bit too much." I mean they're bound to notice, aren't they? You know what Krauts are. Clever.'

'The answer is that if the devaluation had come earlier the Glasgow Company would have asked a higher price. So they haven't lost anything.'

'I don't absolutely believe that.'

'Neither do I. But it's the only answer they're going to get.'

'But won't they say, "Achtung, achtung, Oberlord Sarson, you're up there in high places and that's why we pay you. But you didn't give us the best advice. If you'd wanted you could have saved us."'

'Simple,' Andrew replied. 'Unless they'd had Sarson they never would have got Bank of England permission to buy, anyway. Questions would have been asked in the House, and the whole project would have had to be abandoned.'

Stella sighed: 'How many people knew you were definitely due to pay out today?'

'Only Sarson, Alisdair and me.'

'It's going to happen,' she said with certainty.

'And the cashier,' Andrew said. Then he added, 'But he's president of the regimental dinner club of the East Surrey Brigade.' This was Sarson's disparaging term for his loyal, if clerkly, assistants.

Andrew seemed to hate Stella's silence more than her questions. He said, 'Honestly, darling, it's not a time for Socialistic moral stands and all that. If you're going to react like this I shan't be able to tell you anything.' He looked very anxiously at her, as if to say, 'Be cruel and all the bounce in me will go again.' So she let him off.

Finished drying, she said, 'I don't know if Elizabeth Pitt is all that fantastically beautiful, but the thought of her cool and crisp in clean, white frilly petticoat and summer frock, sitting there with Alisdair amidst the chintzes – that really drives me frantic.'

Chapter 6

It was in an effort to describe the subsequent events and clear her own mind that Stella called on her cousin George on the Sunday evening. She said, 'I hate my husband, George. He's a kind of Tory fellow traveller, d'you know what I mean? I hate his guts, except it's his lack of guts that I object to. . . .' It was, as usual, impossible to tell whether she was serious. She spoke lightly, but she was looking very anxious; her eyes like coals. The shadows under them were deep, her cheeks a creamy white.

'I've just put him on the night train to Glasgow, the same one we eloped on seven years ago when I was young and straight and smooth and more or less untouched by human hand. Dear cousin, I'm feeling sad and a wee bit sick.'

There had been something unsettled, disorganised about the whole week-end, and this sense of confusion persisted, even at George's. As she talked, he kept walking in and out of his gloomy sitting-room collecting glasses, flagons of cider, beer and wine, packets of crisps and a cherry cake (one of which he was sent each month by his mother in Glasgow).

'Ten years as London's leading bachelor,' he said from his kitchen-bathroom, 'has taught me to keep my drink in one room, my visitors in another and my bed in a third.'

Stella kicked off her shoes and sat down on the floor, then leant back on the armchair. She knew she should have offered to help him. She drew up her knees and clasped her hands underneath them. Her skirts always looked short because her legs were so long. She was wearing a brown shirt, made for a man, and when she tipped forward her black slip held her heavy breasts. She rested her chin gloomily on her knees. Her stockings, too, were dark; not exactly netted, but with a criss-cross design. Stella always looked like the most popular girl in the Union; the students' choice.

The room was tidy for a bachelor's but not fastidiously so. Dusted yet dusty, it had the grey Bayswater look of a small salary, no capital and dependants in the provinces, which was more or less George's story. There must be a George in everybody's life; the family friend who likes his independence, but is always willing to baby-sit in a crisis; the only bachelor we know whom we do not suspect of homosexuality. This George was thin with spiky hair and pointed ears. But he had much in common with all the other Georges who perhaps have more time than married people to read the weeklies and form opinions. His comments on political events were sharp and acid, delivered quietly and obscenely; his opinions of other acquaintances, too, were severe, but never bitchy; his account of their activities humorous, perceptive, but never waspish. Underneath his most cruel comments lay a foundation of such tenderness that he could never quite hide it; he could talk rudely and spitefully all night and people still knew that he was kind. His actions often went against what he said. Always criticising Andrew, for instance, for everything from his class to the cut of his coat, he was still one of his most reliable friends. Everybody said he was in love with Stella, but she denied it. If it were true, he kept it to himself. Right underneath he was controlled by a certain temper, which possibly went with some undiscovered constitutional weakness; a kidney that didn't work, a dormant cancer. He had a kind of tender pessimism, the sort that made him believe that he was saying a sensible, not an ill thing, to himself when he swore he would never have children for fear of hurting them.

This evening he was giving a farewell party for friends before going on his first adult seaside holiday, at the age of thirty-six. He was circulation manager of one of the farthest Left weeklies and he had been to both Bournemouth and Blackpool to conferences on behalf of the paper. But he had not taken a holiday, except back to Glasgow to see his mother, for ten years. His friends had therefore more or less forced this, like all his other parties, on him. He said he was only anxious to know how many would bring their own crisps.

As he came back into the sitting-room, Stella said, 'This is an adultery story, that's what it is. There's every sign. . . . No, don't run away, dear, it's not you I have in mind.'

'Thank you,' George said without a smile. 'I confess I am a little disappointed, especially as Andrew's a close friend. Adept adulterers tell me that best friends' wives come high on the list, along with step-mothers and married half-sisters.'

He drifted back to the kitchen again and when he returned Stella had spread herself right across the carpet, face downwards. She was shaking. For a second he thought it was her asthma, but he was only half right.

Sure, then, that she was laughing, he asked, 'What's killing you? Did I say something?'

It was in the sudden way that she shook her head that he realised she was crying. He sat down beside her on the floor, cross-legged, almost formally, orientally, and then slowly pulled her head and shoulders up. She hung on to him desperately, crying and crying, saying only one thing: 'I'm a good girl. I want to be good. I want to be good.' He did not answer or hurry her in any way. He held on to her, provided a handkerchief when at last she asked for one, was unembarrassed by her gusts of tears and sobs, yet did not try to stop them in their course. When at last the storm was over, he fetched her a drink of gin and sat down and listened very seriously.

She said, 'I mean I can see only too clearly how it could become an adultery story – though I can't quite see why. But I'm frightened of the drift. In the old days, if you read Scottish trials you find lots of girls themselves surprised, suddenly raped or murdered before they even notice their boy friend is on the weird side. It's not like that now. We watch ourselves, so we're spectators at every big event except our own funerals. But it doesn't seem to stop us doing bloody stupid things, just the same. All our knowledge seems to do is enable us to see ourselves acting like ignorants.' She took a deep breath. 'Here we go,' she said, 'with the philosophical introduction, part one.'

'Who's the other man?'

'I'll come to him.'

'That Sarson?'

'I said I'll come to him.'

'I was at the christening, don't forget.' She looked at

68

him, puzzled. She had been certain that she gave nothing away that day.

'You read one,' she said, 'a little too well.'

'Was he at the station tonight?'

'Yes.'

'Did he go to Glasgow with Andrew?'

'No.'

'Ah,' George said. 'Ah.'

Then, 'No,' she said again. No, as it were, to the
inevitable. George asked, 'Did he bring you here?'

'Yes. He asked me to supper.'

'You said you preferred sardines with your common
cousin?'

'Exactly.'

'And he said if you get bored, my number's in the
book.'

'Not exactly.'

George thought for a moment.

'Ah,' he said again, understanding, but she checked
him.

'Ah, what?'

'You already knew the number.'

'Go up, George MacNaughten,' she said, leaning her
head back on the arm of the chair, 'to the top of the
class.' She gave him a warm smile, then a moment
later she started to speak again, softly, at first apparently
about something else altogether. But George knew her
mind well, and waited for her to finish and make her
point. As she talked, he made some toast and they ate
it, dry, as they drank. With George, neat gin and dry
toast seemed unexceptional and tasted good.

She said, 'Back at the academy, in our neo-Joycian

69

youth, substituting the I.L.P. for the Holy Ghost, when you must have been about to move down here, long before the great Stella MacNaughten was Dux. . . . Back, back, back down the long alleys in the trams on which you must not spit, let's find me at fourteen, if I was as much as that, my school certificate behind me but I'm still a junior in the flesh. I was standing one day in one of these places in the girl's academy that are difficult to describe, a kind of widening of the corridor where some lockers or some books were kept on shelves. It wasn't big enough to count as a landing or a hall, but in fact it was on the first floor, just near by the entrance to the gallery of the school hall, the room for the speeches and prayers and " I'll see you after, Sarah Todd, I'll *get* you" and all the rest, which we always called Big School. I was talking with some of my girl friends, three or four; if I really strain myself I'm sure I can think of exactly what. I'm blessed with a curious kind of memory.' She waited for a moment, frowning. Then after about ten seconds of concentration it came back to her. 'We were talking about a piece of French translation we had to do that was taken from the weirdest book by George Sand called *La Mare au Diable*, a funny kind of Hogarthian piece it is, and I was going on about George Sand living with Cornel Wilde, a movie that had much impressed me at the local bug-house. . . . All of a sudden a party comes by – centre-piece our dear headmistress who always sat so you could see her suspenders, but had a first in Mods and Greats. She never could quite make up her mind whether I was a prize pupil or a bad influence. This afternoon, I'm neither. We've just been let out of dancing-class which you can see through the glass doors, in Big School, below, and we're on our way to piano practice. We have our music cases – those wallet things with a metal bar at the top, to prove it. The headmistress is showing an important man round: a Glasgow man, apparently, but gone a long way since then. He's been Secretary of State for Air or something and he's got that peach-fed silvery look; he's interested in everything and mentioned in every Duchess's diary from here to New Delhi – you know?'

'I see him,' George said.

'I'm fourteen and a half at most, but he catches my eye and I still feel the colour come up. I'm just praying the headmistress'll stop and say, something: it doesn't matter what, so long as she says "Stella" first. . . .'

She stopped and burrowed in her bag for a cigarette. Then, in clouds of smoke, looking more Bloomsbury than usual, brisker suddenly and as emancipated as a girl can get, she said, 'That, then, is the metaphysics, or the pure physics of the situation. That last sortie goes to describing the elemental factor, which is a prime factor, meaning, if you haven't forgotten your school cert, a factor which you can't analyse any further. This is important. The scene I described in fact took place, some ten years after I suggested in the old building, at Sarsons Browne one day when I was visiting and the Chairman walked by. That the school scene is so vivid may mean that one happened too, but I wouldn't swear to it. But the blush, the blush you can feel right down, is a schoolgirl's blush, either way. A hundred factors may affect what happens to me with regards to Sarson, but in the first place there's X, whatever it is: the old magnet thing felt hard and strong and low, dreamt

71

about, hated, loved, all the rest, and all at this stage purely or impurely in Stella's mind. It is inexplicable except to say that I think that with Sarson it would be like being pinned down by a big panther and evidently I want to be pinned down by a big panther. Let's leave it at that.'

'I think,' George said gently, topping her glass up with gin, 'your point is made.'

She said, this time flatly and vaguely, as if the thought had just occurred to her, 'I don't want to be unfaithful. I really don't. I don't believe in that.' Then she relaxed again and the tense Bloomsbury woman vanished with a flivver of a sigh. She said, 'Just looking at you, I know you're as bad as me. All that progressive party man stuff's a white lie.'

'You'd better be careful.'

'It is, in a way. A real modern Socialist can walk out on her husband. I tell myself I could, but if I did the world would come to an end. Everything I'd ever done would be made meaningless in that moment. I'd lose my confidence even with the kids. That's all laid as deep as Jimmy Maxton. And after today's experience the world seems to be coming to an end.'

She looked up at the clock. 'When are all your guests coming?' she asked, and he resisted following her eyes.

'We've got plenty of time,' he said and there seemed to be something depressing him. She looked at him softly, enquiringly, recognising the note in his voice. He smiled, or rather grinned. George either grinned or remained severe. He touched his head.

He said, 'I've got a little picture here of a bloke

sitting alone by his fireside saying, "so you're not a panther, so what. . . ?"'

She stretched out a hand to his at once and said, 'Oh, come on, Cousin, that's not like you. Why ruin a beautiful honest relationship like ours?'

He put up a warning finger. 'Andrew apart,' he said, 'Andrew apart, let me here and now warn you, if you have a go with that constipated, conceited arrogant Sarson – and you'll tell me, I know – oh, yes, you'll tell me – but if you do, I'm warning you, Andrew apart, I'll be bloody angry.'

'Why?'

'Why?' he echoed loudly and looked up at the ceiling in mock despair. 'For heck's sake, girl, we get done enough by his sort, don't we, without having to go and ask for it? . . . That's exactly what you're doing. It's the old Boot stuff, this. That's clear a mile off. But one of the big ideas is that we should rid ourselves of that kind of behaviour, masochism, all that, then perhaps it'll die out altogether. . . .'

He sounded less certain and she laughed at him. 'It doesn't work,' she said, 'what you're saying doesn't work.'

He answered quite angrily, 'It's still got a lot of truth in it. The housemaid and the Master.'

She bit her lip. 'It'll never happen,' she said. 'If it was going to happen it would have happened by about now. It was all set up.'

'Did you know he was going to be at the station?'

'I thought he was going with Andrew, or Andrew going with him. They've had telephone calls and panics all week-end. Andrew was down at the office this morn-

73

ing – a Sunday, too! Even Sarson can't make a clean decision when it comes to this kind of arrangement. Aeroplanes were booked, cancelled, sleepers, the lot, all because some business men in Paisley want to put their view to an independent party before their conferences with the Germans who are taking them over. In the end Sarson had an unlikely pang of conscience and seeing the Germans were his clients thought it best not to go North without talking to Hamburg first. So his son-in-law Alisdair goes in his place, but as he's not experienced Sarson decides Andrew must go too. He's still talking to Alisdair telling him what to do when we arrive at the train.'

'Then how did you behave?'

'Awful, Cousin, awful. I'd had a running battle with Andrew for twenty-four hours, and we were cold as death at six – death of a marriage, that is. I hardly agree to go to Euston. Then as soon as we meet Sarson I'm all talk and sparkle, like something out of the tennis club at Troon. I'm telling them how Andrew and I went on this train on our elopement, blushing at one minute, being broad as hell the next. Just as common in the nasty coy sense of common as a girl can be. I even jump into the train so Andrew can give me a proper kiss goodbye. I'm shouting to him to behave himself, leaping about the platform, waving as if I'm aching to spend a penny. Oh dear, oh dear, oh dear. It was a terrible performance. I might as well have worn a paper hat.'

'Did Sarson think it so bad?'

'Evidently not.'

'Did Sarson put off the Glasgow trip because –'
She interrupted. 'No.'

'But he was glad you had come to see Andrew off?'

'So he said.'

'And what did you say?'

'I was just stupid. Right down to the "oh reely. I don't know what you mean" level. In fact I was that bit snooty, quoting my supper date with you, my nose in the air, my backside out behind me and my cheeks with that livid glow that only the lights at Euston produce. When he offered me a lift in his taxi I said something I could have kicked myself for. I said, "Thank you, but I don't want a divorce just yet." Can you imagine? Come hither, come hither, said little Miss Muffet.' And she added, 'I'm perfectly certain she did, by the by; spiders don't just sit down beside you. That's fact.'

George was frowning thoughtfully. He chewed some dry toast. Then he said, 'But you knew his telephone number?'

'Yes. I've been to his flat.'

George looked at her with raised eyebrows.

'I told you. No,' she said.

'But you describe this Euston scene in prickly detail and if you're telling the truth I swear you've never talked to him before.'

She nodded. 'That's true,' she said. 'But it's the scene, not the account of it, that was false. . . . It's always a bit like that when I meet him. I'm "kitten", like any other office wife, but tonight I think the station or the size of him did something for me even when the others left. I think maybe I was really frightened I was going to say "No, no, no, don't please, don't call a

75

cab, Mr Bovary, no, no, no, not that." So in self-defence I remembered you. Isn't that a compliment?'

'No,' George rightly replied. 'It's the tragedy of my life.'

He went to answer the 'phone which rang and made her jump. It was one of his guests who had forgotten the way. Looking at Stella all the time, he patiently gave the directions. Then he put the receiver down softly. He certainly could read her.

'You gave him this number?' he asked. She was already blushing.

'I told you it was bad.'

He sat down on the floor again. He said, 'About the row with Andrew' – and at once she answered, 'Yes, well done. That better be aired. Rows not row, really, I suppose. Except all rows in marriage are the same row, if one boils them down far enough.' She frowned. 'I think that's true.' But before she went back to the rows with Andrew she suddenly sat up and said, 'George, that prime factor. The magnetic thing. I know maybe it's no good trying to factorise it any further but do you think with somebody like me falling that hard, it isn't quite what you said, I mean not boot-licking and that, but the opposite – the feeling that in a Sarson's world a Sarson's what a girl must get. And because it's such a Darwinian, Sarsonian set-up and has been for years and years now, I feel the attraction at the bottom of my spine, not merely a cerebral and prudent attraction any more. That, primarily?'

But George was not going to be drawn on the subject. He said, 'Or it could be just because he's the farthest out of reach. I think you were right before. You can't factorise a prime number. Yen is yen. Only it gets worse if for lots of other reasons we want to think about it too much. Be a bachelor for a long time: if you're going to be happy you have to be one ahead of your appetites. Either that or wind up in the nude clubs, or wolfing the streets. Why I'm asking you, "What about the rows?" is not to find out anything about your yen for Sarson, which I'm taking for granted. All I want to know is why you're indulging it.'

'The way you say "indulge" reminds me of John Knox.'

George nodded, 'And very right, too. Let's have some sort of account of a week-end with Andrew.'

'Yes, I want to tell you that, for a reason which'll come later, but another thing, because you're one of the only ones that would understand how it all began. I won't go into the details, because I swore I wouldn't, but Sarsons are obviously –'

'Sarson man or Sarson firm?'

'Both really, up to the hilt in a racket, or so it would seem. And I don't joke. A real scandal, just the thing your editors would go wild about, if they could publish without libel. Anyway Andrew's spotted this, or he thinks he's spotted it. He'll know sometime next week. He's quite unshocked, a little surprised and excited as he tells me, but *accepting* it – I promise! I suppose it's what we've said before – something to do with hating the English,' she said more wildly. 'I don't think he's got that in him, the way we have. So there he is, witness to a massive Tory double-deal and he just sits and takes it. Not that he's involved. I think that might almost be better. He'd get a cut. But he's got himself in the position of seeing no evil.'

George was careful to be fair. He asked, 'Maybe for the same reason as usual – that it hurts if you do see too much. Has he been frightened lately?'

'He'd been *piano*.'

'Have you been going at him?'

'Not until yesterday. It was on Friday night he told me all this, and I danced a war dance, but he wouldn't tell me what he was going to do, if it is proved beyond reasonable doubt that the racket exists. Of course, on the Saturday, when I've had time to think of this, I'm dead excited right down inside, you know. I feel this is what I've been waiting for all my life, a real splendid example which he and I could brew up; we'd get you and the rest and we'd strike a splendid blow just when one's needing struck. But George, either we're mad or he is. Sometimes when he's excited he'll get what he calls "committed", which means he'll talk politics for two minutes; he'll even say that all's not as it should be, but he's no more committed than all these actors you meet who talk wildly Left thinking they'll get into a bright Company that way. You know, it doesn't really catch him by the spine. With Glasgow people like you and me politics is part of it, isn't it? It's life, from hot tears in a corner to a Sunday outing with some ridiculous flag, Sister Anna and the rest – but not for Andrew. With him politics is a thing apart. You could drop an atomic bomb on Berlin and he still would have to pretend he's keen to vote. . . .'

George hugged his knees and answered, calmly, 'You knew all this before. If you didn't you must be blind.'

'Of course I did.' She nodded and replied softly, 'I knew it when we met in the only pub where a girl could go to in Oxford in those days. Gee, that's an age back. It had a funny mixed clientele, that pub. . . . Emancipated beer-drinkers like me and cloth caps and beagles there as well. No wonder we love Oxford, and don't look at me like that. I know I'll never interest you, but it's still vivid for me just the same. Andrew and I have got that in common. Our lovers' myth. We both went in there for lunch one day in the vacation when he was pretending to work, and I was really working. He'd no idea of how to work, but he wanted to learn. That was the difference between him and all the sweet-looking morons and cherubs that were his beetle-crushing friends. I knew then he was bored with politics and he was meant to be studying them. War and history would entertain him but the idea of a movement, Fabian or anything else, or the first smell of trouble in the Labour party that was brewing just then – these things left him colder than cold. Yet he was more excited about living, saying "yes" to life more often to the hour than anybody else I'd ever met, that in the end I began to think it was me that was silly to be concerned and for months, even years, I really lived it that way. Like everybody else, I suppose, until Suez, when Andrew – I watched him – changed sides half-way through: he was still under the Churchillian clouds when it started, then he kept his ears open, and he went with the brighter boys in the City, arguing like mad at dinner parties, sleeping dreamlessly at nights. I'm telling you I knew all along. I didn't know I was setting out to say it, so you've helped, but it seemed that when he was answering "yes" to everything, when he was all energy, his political blank didn't matter. Now he's changed, he's still saying "yes" but in a different way.'

'How much has he changed?'

She answered doubtfully, 'Not too much. But yesterday he was pretending to be seriously concerned and he was secretive all day, even at dinner – we went out. Then the host kept plying him with drinks and the pose was a bit too much for him so he started giggling and playing the fool and grabbing the centre of the stage. It's one thing or the other, and I must admit I like him better when he's most annoying, asking questions and answering them himself – interrupting, all the rest. But just as he can be bright and childish like that, he can be cruel too, my Andrew.'

George listened closely to this. He had never heard her speak of it before. She seemed to be counting her fingertips as she went on, 'He can be very nasty, verbally I mean, very terrible, very swiftly. It would almost be better if he lammed me one.'

'How exactly?'

'I can't tell you exactly, Cousin, because I don't want to remember. I don't want to remember first because it hurts, which is cowardice, but second for what at least I tell myself is a better reason. Because he doesn't mean the things he says like that, not anyway against me, he means them against himself, but he happens to lash out at his twin, for if you marry young enough you've got to be wife and twin sister as well. When he says he wants to be rid of me I know very well, or I have persuaded myself to believe, that he's saying something in a way more terrible, not less. Saturday night was suddenly very bad. I think he was hating himself for being quite inadequate to cope with this office thing. He didn't have any morals, any courage, even any opinion when it came to it and so he really let fly at me, because weak I may be but not weak in that way. Yet I believe in a real crisis, an old-fashioned one like war or plague, Andrew would be good. He wouldn't claim that for himself. But I know it's true. Andrew's a good person, underneath. He loves, George. Andrew loves.'

They were interrupted then, by the arrival of the first guests, and because George was himself always faultlessly polite, she did not try to leave at once.

The party was bigger than she had expected. The place was soon packed with ageing jazzmen and perpetual students who all seemed to have attachments to weekly journals, children in St. John's Wood or Haverstock Hill, and time to drink in Soho in the afternoons. They lay about talking, drinking and smoking and only three of the couples bothered to dance. Most of them soon forgot that the purpose of this spontaneous party was to celebrate George's holiday. There was a rather disturbingly passive note in the performance. A rowdier spirit might have been expected from people who were, one and all, committed to the Left. But there seemed to be invisible cobwebs hanging between many of the couples. They looked at the door even as they talked to each other, as if they were waiting for somebody else who was important to them. George came up and danced with Stella, then sat for a moment, holding her hand.

'Can we get you something?'

'No thanks, I'm fine, George.' She had become a Glasgow girl again.

'More gin?'

'No.'

'Be fair –' But she shook her head. 'Can I introduce you to one of these erupted rams?'

'No thanks.' She looked like a girl being cheerful over whisky and sandwiches after a funeral.

Not much later, she left, unnoticed. She did not wander away, then have second thoughts, then see a telephone. From the moment she closed the door behind her she was like a totally different girl. She ran downstairs, ran into the street, walked fast, hurried, ran until she saw somebody and, as if a house were on fire, asked him where there was a telephone nearby. She knew Sarson had a mistress; she thought he would not sleep alone; she knew it was getting late. She had to run from the kiosk to a little café to get some change for the box. She had kept pennies all evening, prepared for this, but the box would not swallow one of them. Again, the people in the next door café thought there must be some sort of emergency. For two seconds they all looked up from their cups of tea as the proprietor enquired. Then with a new penny she ran back to the 'phone again. When at last she got through she was in a hopeless state of tension. She was heaving with asthma, battered and burnt by pain. She could say little more than, 'I'm stuck. Sarson, I'm stuck.'

'But where are you?'

'I don't know,' she paused, trying to get her breath.

'Tell me where, I'll come.'

'It's a box. It's at a big cross-roads.'

'Near where you went for supper?'

'Yes. I'm not really ringing you, I –'

'Wasn't that Elgin Gardens?'

She seemed astounded that she should have given so much away already.

'Yes.'

'Did you walk into London or out? D'you remember which direction?'

'Sort of in.'

'Stay exactly where you are. Good girl. I won't be five minutes.'

He sounded quite calm and the receiver was replaced. When he came she was still in the kiosk and she hugged him very tightly. She spoke in a muddled way about Mary, Queen of Scots. She was trying to say that she understood her better now. Had there been an attractive girl at George's she would have liked to have gone to bed with her, not Sarson at all. In the taxi she managed at last to get that across. Mary never slept alone: not from Rizzio's murder until the night after Carberry Hill. 'In strain,' she said, 'choose your own sex. There's no commitment there.' Then she wiped her hair from her brow and calmed down a little. 'Will that awful Salmon of yours be there watching?'

'No,' he said, 'there's nobody in the flat.'

'I don't care who's watching.' She surprised herself with the reply. The streets, outside, looked black and shiny and damp. She felt small; like the girl with the music case, and her name had been called. Wee tart, Stella. That's what you are, Stella Vass.

Part Two

Chapter 7

At half past five Andrew had tottered out of his sleeper into the hotel in Glasgow, and Alisdair had the neighbouring room. But the hotel was notorious for insomnia. Immediately outside the bedroom windows a lady with a low and soothing Glasgow voice announced local train departures to Renfrew, Paisley, Lockerbie and Carlisle, at irregular intervals. Each plug that was pulled in nearby lavatories burst like a grenade in Andrew's eardrum. He could hear travellers' teeth fall with a clink into bedside glasses, four floors above.

At eight o'clock a maid who seemed to have been chosen as much for her ugliness as her respectability brought in a huge breakfast tray with tea, toast, jelly marmalade, a big plate of orange-coloured bacon and eggs and some egg-coloured orange juice. At once Andrew grabbed the newspaper.

The room was very big, with terrible Victorian furniture. It was occupied only by salesmen, these days, but it had seen better days when richer children had come up from the country at Christmas time to see pantomimes. There was an ornate plaster ceiling and a dusty candelabra. The bedstead itself was splendid, in brass. The rest had somehow crumbled into Gideon and management's regrets.

Sarson was never less than one ahead. There was no devaluation: no new chancellor's announcement, no suggestion of a currency change. The paper was filled with news of the crisis in Algiers.

The architecture and acoustics of the hotel eliminated any element of surprise which might have accompanied Alisdair's arrival from the next-door room. He had read the same newspapers, but more thoroughly. His mood seemed to be tentative but very serious.

'You've seen the papers?'

Cheerfully Andrew replied, 'I'm sure you've heard I've seen the papers.' Then looking at Alisdair's face he covered himself. 'At least I've seen the front page.' Alisdair nodded, unfolding the paper he was carrying.

'I meant, actually, the financial news.'

'I didn't see —'

'The Deutschmark.'

Andrew looked at him and waited.

'Well, frankly what one might expect, if that's not a slanderous thing to say. It's revalued,' Alisdair said.

'How much?'

'Up fifteen per cent.' Alisdair folded up his paper again. Andrew was pouring himself another cup of tea.

Alisdair said, '£675,000, I think, is the answer that you're looking for.'

Andrew made a wry face, and they were both quiet for a moment. They avoided each other's eye as if suddenly they weren't quite sure where the other stood. £675,000 was the profit to Sarsons Browne, thanks to the delay in conversion.

When Alisdair said, 'Look, I want to talk to you,' Andrew nodded, but this was one of the few times in his life when he would have preferred to skip a discussion. He saw very well what had happened, but now, when he should at once come to a decision, there was a curious lag. What was happening was that he instinctively realised the danger of taking one side or the other, even if he did not calculate quite why. The butterfly game which he had played all his life had come sharply to an end. He had to face himself, for the first time, in the lobby. He had to walk through one door or the other, and Stella was right, the really worrying thing was that he did not care which. If somebody had whispered in his ear, 'Stick to Sarson and you'll make £1,000 a year more, on average,' he might have swayed that way, and not felt too badly about it. Dumbly, he listened to Alisdair, who resembled the bomber pilot of twenty years before as he broached the subject. He pulled out a packet of cigarettes and said, 'Please don't try to put me off.'

The Sunningdale expression which goes with open cars went also, in the war, with dashing leadership; and the Few, when it came to the push, showed a surprising, springy steeliness. So it was with Alisdair. His eyes, particularly, changed to a harder sort of green, belonging to an older man. This reserve of strength no doubt accounted for the wins at squash at the Lansdowne, but nobody in Sarsons Browne had seen it until now.

Andrew was surprised, even rather alarmed by it. He spoke facetiously, East Surrey-wise, about the profit on the Deutschmarks. 'Maybe when we return the headmaster will give us a half hol,' he said.

Alisdair turned round by the window. He was wearing a silk dressing-gown and he leant back on the radiator. As he talked he drummed his thin fingers against it and there was a clink each time it was struck by his chunky signet ring.

'Andrew, don't talk like that. You know how serious

I am. I didn't mention this before because I wasn't sure –'

'You're still not *sure* – ' Andrew said.

Alisdair nodded then lit his cigarette. He started to go through the whole process as they had witnessed it. He did this now for the first time, but over the next two days while they were in Glasgow they must have gone through it a hundred times, remembering every syllable the Chairman had uttered on the Friday afternoon. Each time Andrew appeared to strengthen in Alisdair's favour. But the movement could be described differently. Andrew could also have been said to weaken in his support for Sarson.

'I may have got it back to front,' Alisdair began characteristically, with a kind of unbending modesty, 'and knowing my masterly grasp of the inessentials I should think I probably have. In which case, I'd be grateful if you'd put me right.'

After a pause in which to collect his thoughts he went on carefully, 'It's my understanding that the court of the Bank of England advise the Chancellor about anything like devaluation.'

'We didn't devalue,' Andrew corrected him.

'I'm coming to that. Am I right in the first instance? '

Andrew would not have remembered this sort of fact if he had studied it, but having worked in the City for seven years, he knew the answer well. He lay back against the hard bolsters provided by the hoteliers of a hardy race. 'Not exactly right.'

Alisdair was surprised. 'But surely –'

'Not the whole court. Not necessarily. Quite likely a sub-Committee of the directors; two or three of the permanent servants, one or two of the others. A kind of inner circle. They then recommend action to Downing Street.'

'Is Sarson on that?'

'It varies. He sometimes is. One goes to Washington, another grouse-shooting – somebody else steps in.'

'I think we can *take* it Sarson's in the inner circle of everything in the City,' Alisdair said and again Andrew qualified.

'We can't *take* it. And we probably can never find out. . . .'

'Andrew, don't try and dodge,' he said. 'We both *know*.' Then he went on, 'What passes between you and me here need never come out. It's pointless talking unless we do so frankly. This is terribly important to me. I want to talk it out but take it that nothing you say here can be quoted in evidence against you. It's a private chat.'

How wrongly, with a nod, Andrew agreed. Then for an hour and a half, like a dog who would not drop a bone, Alisdair kept worrying the problem.

'Frankly,' Alisdair said, 'it's the order of things which gets me.'

'Yes –'

'Otherwise I could swallow it. But, when was it? About the beginning of February when the Hamburg meetings were over, and we'd had the do with the boys up here. When we started setting up the programme. . . . First week of Feb., am I right?'

'Right.'

'Now at that time we put the whole timetable down.'

'For our own use,' Andrew said, almost obstinately. 'It's not an official programme.'

'For our own use. But that doesn't alter the fact. From the first week in March we knew that if things didn't go wrong, if the proofs of the letter didn't get lost, if the G.P.O. didn't go on strike, if the Glasgow boys didn't get cold feet . . . if, if, if . . .' He broke off. 'For Heaven's sake, when the printed envelopes went wrong you had to stay up half the night to see the offer got posted. At that time we fussed enough if a day were lost. Remember the long lecture Sarson delivered? All the spoof about banking and farming or whatever it was . . . "Programmes are there to be kept, not to be ignored. If you're late on the last of the hay you may not be in a position to cope with the first of the wheat. . . ."'

Andrew nodded. It was true.

So Alisdair now pressed on. 'Fine, so we all know what he feels about the programme and last Friday's date for despatch of cheques, which means the last moment for exchange of Marks has been fixed for jolly nearly two months. So now on Friday morning, off he goes down the road to Threadneedle Street for the cricket scores.'

'La, la, la, la –'

'– And back by two o'clock. So, what do we talk about? You heard. And at the week-end, yesterday, we talked about salmon going up river when we met. Yes! we did! For Christ's sake, Andrew, all he's got to do on Friday afternoon is sign a couple of chits, but no, suddenly, very casual-like he wants a day off. And then you – I'd say myself as well, only I'm so bloody dim I miss half of what's going on and can't open my mouth when he's in the vicinity – so you lower your eyelashes and say "why not tarry awhile?" and so we all jog off home for a comfy week-end. Bingo, Sunday night the Krauts make this revaluation statement, and here we are on Monday morning. . . . And, honestly, I don't like it, Andrew. I'm talking very seriously, I don't know what the technical difference between evidence and circumstantial evidence is but, commonsense-wise, I'm going to take a lot of persuading to believe that on Friday at lunch the gentlemen did not discuss the German Deutschmark. Could they know?' He shrugged. 'Of course I know they could. . . . I mean *how* could they know?'

Andrew put his breakfast tray to one side. 'It's damned unlikely they'd know, though I believe any substantial change in currency has to be announced in advance to the International Monetary Fund. How they enforce that's something different.'

'That's enough. The Governor would be warned, and therefore his staff. Oh, my God . . .' Alisdair said. 'It's like death or murder or any of these things. Your accident all over again,' he added, and Andrew put a hand on his stomach in protest. 'One simply can't believe it happens to oneself. There's always rumour of privilege in the City but one somehow never associated it with Sarsons. Do the other gentlemen know, one wonders? Or is there a kind of blinkers rule, so the member banks are like a gents' lavatory and nobody looks over the stalls? They just hear whispers and ignore them. . . .'

He threw his cigarette out the window, greatly to the danger of the first commuters below, but he did not even notice what he had done. He said with a sigh, more like himself again, 'I don't say I'll do anything, I haven't got the guts to, probably. Anyway, he's my father-in-law. There's Elizabeth to think about as well. It's going to suit me in the end, of course it is, but I'd like to know. I feel like Midshipman Hawkins. "Look here, sir, just tell me one thing, sir, is this a pirate vessel or a sloop in the service of the King's Navee?"' They both laughed at the parallel. Andrew was relieved by this last speech of Alisdair's; it was possible that no action would be taken.

'It bloody well smells to high heaven, that's what it does,' Alisdair said, then he turned back to Andrew and asked, 'Doesn't it?'

Andrew swung his feet out of bed and stared at his toes: he was cagey again. 'I wasn't at the lunch in Threadneedle Street.'

But Alisdair shook his head slowly. Just before he left the room he said again the one thing which somehow irreversibly suggested action against Sarson.

'We know, Andrew, we *know*.'

Chapter 8

They did not sleep in the double room which Sarson used when his wife was up in London. Instead, they spent a couple of hours of passion and four of discomfort in Sarson's single bed. His little room with the roll-top desk in the window was gloomily overfurnished and smelt, correctly, of shoes, shoe polish, papers, mothballs, Trumper's Isis water and all things male.

Stella was not woken in any romantic way. She heard her name called several times and not in a friendly tone. She sat up with a shock, pretending to herself that she did not know where she was. There was a sound of running water in the distance. Sarson was shouting from the bathroom. 'If you want a bath, there's one running for you now.'

He did not leave his water in for her. He presumably imagined that she did not want to use it. Sarson's was a prefect's sex life; secretive, necessary, repetitive, regretted and lonely. He did not wait in the bathroom, nor return to his own room until she had left it. He seemed purposely to avoid her at this hour, yet the night had been a success. All women, at breakfast time, were a drag. With the superior air of a proficient scout he prepared breakfast, put it on trays and carried it into the sitting-room, which got its only hour of sunshine at this time. The brown egg from the country in solid silver egg-cup, the sun, and the honey in the honeycomb persuaded Stella to stay, when at last she emerged from the bath-room. Sarson himself gave her no encouragement beyond a little smile and nod, as he lowered the ordinary *Times*. The pink one was kept for the journey into the City.

At breakfast Stella was actually trying to factorise Sarson's X. She used the form the Romans never categorised; a girl talking, expecting neither the answer yes or no.

'These brown eggs and you all shaved and uncommunicative remind me of the seductive literature I used to read but never told my teachers.' The newspaper was not lowered, but she did not seem to care. 'I used to read the right things to get a scholarship on, like *Animal Farm* and *The Castle*, but for pleasure I used to read those high-class ladies that wrote between the wars about their own affairs, thinly-disguised in near poetic prose. The last of the potting-shed school, with unrequited love, midges, pigeons, twilight, country houses, rooky woods and purring, powerful cars. Uncommunicative heroes called Rollo and Max, shadowy and upper class and with ivory hair brushes just like yours. Oh, dear, the indulgence of that! Re-reading was like swimming in warm water. Mind, they agreed with my teachers in one thing. The affairs in the end were always empty and bad and sad. The heroine could only write a book. The authoress, I fancied, had that bombed-out look by then, travelling down, alone, by first-class train to see her son win the hundred yards sprint.' She looked up at Sarson who was now eating bread and honey. She said, 'They weren't half right about the hero being uncommunicative. Have you got a soul, Sarson?'

'Not at breakfast time.'

'Oh, you big Tom.'

After that he read out an extract of a review of a new

96

play which he thought was clever and she did not listen to it.

She said, 'The delicious, exciting relationship which exists between us two this morning reminds me of co-education. There was an age when we and the boys played it adult. We would sensibly discuss anything you like and remarkably frankly. Not that we'd persuade each other to each other's views. That would be too undignified. Touching too was quite out. The surface of the skin was neither plus nor minus for attraction or repulsion, but strictly neutral. But then you missed out on co-education.'

He smiled tolerantly, licked his thumb, stood up, stretched and then looked at his watch.

'I must go and shit,' he said. The sun had warmed him. 'Salmon's driving up. I don't expect he'll be long now.'

She said, amazedly, 'I'm wondering what you think I am. D'you know you're in danger of getting this fresh country butter in your eye?'

He stood looking down at her and said, 'I think he'll be about ten minutes.'

'Oh, dear,' she said; then with sarcasm, 'D'you want me to wash my dishes or change the sheets?'

Perfectly seriously he answered, 'Oh, no, I'll do that. It might be better, though, if –'

'If I hoofed it.'

He looked at her angrily for a second and her courage failed her. She said so meekly that she scarcely recognised herself, 'I'm not really complaining. I'll go quietly, gov.'

'I wish I could ask you to stay.'

He retired to the bathroom, with *The Times*, closed but did not lock the door and settled there, as if for a long time. She collected her coat and shouted good-bye from the hall.

'Bye-bye, Stella,' he said in quite a friendly way, from the bathroom, as if a teen-aged daughter was going off for the day.

Descending in the lift, with her hands jammed in her pockets, her hair pushed back from her face with a flick of her head, she smelt the pile of the carpet and after an uneasy moment decided to laugh at herself, not cry.

She knew exactly why she then indulged herself by going about Mayfair doing those things which as a little girl she had always imagined she would do: the things that women do in the provinces, but only strangers do in London. She looked at expensive goods in shops, and had some cake with a big cup of white coffee at half past ten in Fullers. She went to a bookshop and bought a nice easy bestseller about sex and rain and God which she knew she would never finish. But the book itself, the jacket, the hard boards and the smell of the paper reminded her of days when she had said to herself, 'I shall do that, when I grow up.'

The desire to relegate herself, to allow herself to become the sort of acceptance person who did with enjoyment the things she was doing about London this morning was very strong. She could see all her own contemporaries, all the Maggies and Grizels in Glasgow and Aberdeen, married happily to big husbands on good salaries, giggling in coffee shops, in big department stores, gossiping about age, about hats, about eccentric acquaintances, always with good humour. She envied them now. But she knew that the picture of herself in that role was as much an illusion as literary seduction with midges.

One indulges a child after a disappointment. A bicycle for a scholarship, but for a failure, a day like this, in town. She felt like the suicide who flings himself off a ledge only to find, as in the best defenestrations, that there is a large dung heap below. Slightly soiled, faintly ashamed of her previous unbalanced and melodramatic view of this sort of night, she caught a number 13 bus back to Golders Green and changed there for Temple Fortune.

But the morning had its crisis. It came suddenly, and her hectic reaction surprised and disturbed her. It was as if she had stretched out one of her limbs as usual but failed to sense what she had touched; immediately aware of some dangerous root paralysis, some fatal flaw in her central nervous system, she reached out again, the second time, felt what she touched, told herself she was reassured, but was little less alarmed.

The actual incident was less dramatic: indeed it was the sort of thing that happens to every housewife ten times a week. Collecting David from his nursery school she walked into the little changing room at the back where the children put on their coats and awful caps. David saw her, let out a cry of delight and came rushing across. But the mistress who was in charge – no more than a girl herself – did not see Stella and she turned swiftly on David, giving him a row, telling him not to shout and to listen to what was being said, for she had been making some announcement at the time.

It was a perfectly understandable mistake. As soon as the girl saw Stella she stopped and apologised. But by then it was too late. Stella had lost her temper, in that instant. As she was twice as beautiful, a head taller, five years older and about ten times more intelligent than the poor young mistress, it was not very difficult for her. She would have reduced her to tears in front of the children had not the owner of the nursery school heard the shouting and come through to see what was wrong. Stella then stopped but refused to go into explanations. She just buttoned up David's coat and without looking either of the women in the eye kept saying, 'Forget it! Forget it!' She tried to make friends with some of David's pals then, calling them by their christian names which she was good at remembering. But they were alarmed by her and answered only in frightened mono-syllables. There was complete silence in the dark little room that smelt of Wellington boots and dried London mud, when she and David left. David was very quiet.

She went past an electrician's shop on the way home and in the window there was a bargain second-hand television set at twenty guineas. Stella had no money of her own but she and Andrew worked on a joint account which they both knew was a mistake. She walked into the shop and five minutes later the deal was done. The television set was to be sent down to the school with the note of apology and good wishes to the 'staff'. She thought it was a pity that strawberries had not been in the shops. She would have sent strawberries and cream to staff and pupils, and that would have been a lot cheaper.

At home, she was more than polite to Elsa and gave

her the novel she had bought, then cooked a good lunch for them all with sausages. But just as she was sitting down to it there was an annoying telephone call.

'Mrs Vass?' in a sing-song voice, was followed by two minutes of silence.

'Mrs Vass? Thank you.'

She thought it might be a call from Glasgow. But it was a secretary calling her from Threadneedle Street – not Sarsons Browne. Mr Sarson was in a meeting at present but hoped she could manage lunch at the Ecu de France, in Jermyn Street, at quarter to two. The secretary asked if there was any reply.

'Thank you,' was all she said. Then she replaced the receiver. Ten seconds later she looked at her watch and realised that if she hurried she could just make it. She ran upstairs to change.

Chapter 9

The back streets in Camden Town are misty and lonely
at dawn, like Flemish streets. The only people about
walk singly, still half asleep, with the glazed look which
honest men must have when they are led to the gallows.
Taxi-drivers have big coats with fur collars fit for Dilke
or Randolph Churchill and coughs that can only lead to
the grave. It is as if one century wakes before the next. It
takes an hour with all the bakers, the sparrows, the
lorries and the rattle of the milk carts before the twen-
tieth century re-awakens. Through these streets, on the
Wednesday morning came Andrew. He did not know
that he arrived home only an hour after Stella who had
come straight from Sarson's bed.

She was always shy of reunions. For the first hour she
would talk sixteen to the dozen and find it hard to look
him in the face. Her behaviour that morning did not,
therefore, surprise him in the least. It was not unusual,
and it never failed to excite him. It was as if by talking
and turning her head she was both running away and
leading him on. They were always in bed together within
an hour of his return from a trip like this. He had hoped
to surprise her there, still warm and naked. He planned
to get under the covers himself, still dressed, dusty and
smelling of travels and train. There was nothing wrong
with Andrew's sexual imagination. But then he never
knew if Stella and he were the most sophisticated
operators in town, or merely children playing at honeymoons.

She was not in bed. She was out in the garden and Josh and David were with her, batting about like mad butterflies in the dew. He said hello to them first, then turned to her. The suggestion of shortness of breath as he approached her delighted him, and he was only encouraged by the expression of apprehension that crossed her face. He said, at once, 'I've made a new resolution. I'm not going to be bloody to Stella any more.'

She nodded and kissed him, and hugged, and he kissed her again, insisting on her mouth. Then quickly she grabbed his hand and held up the spade which she had dug in the earth nearby. Her first sally was as complicated as usual. 'Hello, dear heart, we've missed you. We've reached a kind of Tolstoyan extreme here with faith and the spade –' But he was still repenting, with a smile. 'I can even back it. A lot's happened. It's not just a resolution out of thin air. I won't even be bloody when I'm drunk; no need, any more.'

'Good for you.' She talked loudly, drawing the children in. 'Our spade broke. I got this one next door. They're away, but I don't think they'd mind, do you? . . . I wouldn't mind if someone went to my tool-shed and borrowed a spade, that's if I had a tool-shed. I'm sure that's how Henrietta Barnet, worthy founder, meant it to be. In Haifa and the Ukrainian steppes and places like that people wouldn't think twice about it.'

Andrew now played the understanding husband, allowing her time to settle. He smiled fondly. 'If you go on about it, I'll think you're guilty.'

'A-huh,' she said and stopped for a second. The silence

was curious. Rolling down her sleeves, she started again, indicating the extraordinary hole. 'Isn't it good?' and Josh said solemnly, 'It's a hundred thousand feet deep.'

'Not quite, dear,' she corrected. 'Though I'm not against exaggeration, in principle, I'm not.' She turned back to Andrew. 'Daddy will tell you how deep it is.'

'Daddy,' Andrew replied, somehow this morning, playing with more weight, 'can only say he's out of his depths.'

'It's really not so crazy,' she assured him and sent the boys in to wash their hands before breakfast. Obediently, they left. She said, then, like a Scotch wife, 'You'll be hungry, too, dear.'

He shook his head. 'Not for bacon and eggs.'

She looked quickly back at the hole. 'It should be five foot six. Is it five foot?'

'Four foot.' Andrew guessed and touched her.

She shook her head, but did not move away. She simply ignored the movement of the hand on her hip. 'Mind that's not bad, we only started yesterday evening. We've been in touch with David's friends in the Civil Defence again. It's the only thing that gets him, except corgis, and you can hear too much about them. . . . Gum-boots aren't the best thing for digging,' she added.

Andrew grinned. 'To be absolutely frank,' he replied, 'I think they're the best thing about the digging. Please can I see you in them alone.'

'Twice I've near lost my toe. What was Glasgow like? It's blasphemous you going up to Glasgow without me, nothing else.'

'I want to see you in them alone,' he said disappointedly.

'What have you been thinking about in that train?'

'The idea of you being naked and me not. What were you digging for? Resentment against Andrew, I'll bet. Were you digging with resentment?'

'No,' she replied, 'I told you, it's a question of Civil Defence.'

'One of the best things about you is that you never harbour grievances.'

She shoved her hair back from her forehead with the back of her hand and then suddenly took his arm tightly. She said, 'Here, come round the estate with me, I noticed something fine today. Somewhere at the back here between the privet and the broken Triang milk lorry there's a spectacular golden daffodil.'

They walked slowly the twenty paces to the end of the lawn, and at last she began to explain. 'It's not a hole, incidentally. It's a slit. A slit-trench, to be accurate. The narrowness is part of the thing. . . . Tell me, d'you remember the day I came down and saw you in the City?' And as she said so, she thought, 'how easy it is to lie'. Before he could answer she mentioned something she had seen the afternoon before. 'D'you know that little space of ground with a statue of God-knows-who, that place where we parted from George that day, after lunch?'

'Outside the Royal Exchange?'

'Exactly,' she said and then she pointed to the ground. 'There's the daffodil, by the by.' They started to slow march back to the house.

'I thought about it,' she went on, 'and I worked it

out that if I were Mr Khrushchev, I'd drop the bomb just there, right outside the Royal Exchange. Not on the Bank of England. After all, there are public servants in there. Not on Lloyds, because what about that Stock Exchange? Not on Lazards, because what about Hambros'. . . . All those things. Anyway, I believe for the alpha results with the hydrogen bomb you want to land it on an opening, not inside a big building. There it is then, the heart of European Capitalism: that little patch outside the Royal Exchange.'

Andrew nodded. He said, 'What are you going to cook us for breakfast?'

She looked hurt. She said, 'You mustn't interrupt like that. It's important, this. Because Davie and I went down to the Civil Defence people and we said, "What about this if it is dropped on or near the Bank? What's the chance of survival here on the fringe of the fall-out from the Crematorium?" There was a man there, with a whistle and a badge and it turns out he's an ex-skipper from the Royal Mail Line and very pleased I'd dropped in. He'd been to some course up in Harrogate and he's damned certain the Yanks are wasting money. He enjoys that thought, too, you can tell. . . . He says these expensive shelters are neither here nor there if you're in the area, and if you're out of the area all you need's a slit-trench with three feet of earth piled on top, maybe on a piece of corrugated iron. "The best thing you can do, my dear," he said, "is to dig in like Tommy did in 1914." After that we worked out with a compass just how far away we were from the Royal Exchange, as the crow flies, or the fall-out falls.'

Again Andrew smiled, but he was no longer listening.

In the bright sunlight he could see down on her cheek that he had not known to exist. He touched it and she said, 'I'm going to give the kids their breakfast.'

'Elsa's already doing so.'

'Myself, I'm starving,' she said at the door and started to pull off her gum-boots.

'No, do keep them on, darling, I –'

'And get the whole house covered in mud? Don't be daft –'

'I don't care if we get the whole bed covered in mud,' but he 'helped' her take them off then, running his hands up to her thighs. She suddenly sat very still and stared at him, her eyes black, coal-like, her expression sulky. He was moving his hands very tentatively up to her hips looking at her warily, almost obliquely, like a pony. He had no idea what was going on in her head. He stopped and said disappointedly, 'Not if you don't want to.'

At once she stood up and looked him in the eye with the same hard, puzzled resentment. Then she said, 'I'll just see they're all right, first,' and barefoot, she walked into the kitchen where Elsa was supervising the feast of cornflakes. She poured a cup of tea in a huge breakfast cup and with a sniff, but without explanation, went upstairs. Not very much later, when she had opportunity to finish her tea which she had laid on the bedside table, she was amazed by herself, quite stunned by the contradictions of guilt. She had seldom in her life been so carried away by passion.

Andrew was practically purring with a warm and complacent, but not uncharming, pride. He said, 'I told you everything had changed.'

She drank her tea, and when he asked if he could finish it, she flattered him by saying, 'No, you can't. I need it.'

'You haven't asked me more. Are you just being tactful?'

She seemed quite mystified. 'I was never tactful in my life. I was taught tact's like taste – it saps a girl.' She looked back at him. 'Is there something nasty building up?'

'There is.'

'Are you walking out on me?'

'No.'

'Any clues?'

'You can guess, can't you?'

Still she was mystified. 'The Deutschmark thing.' At once she blushed, and he laughed as he said,

'Do you mean to say you didn't notice?'

She bit her lip and said vaguely, and with a sort of shame, 'Go down to the bottom of the class. I can't have been reading those things I ought to have read.' As she added, 'Dux to dunce in three days,' she thought, 'one thing the double life does do is destroy the data girl. We always give ourselves away.' But Andrew had not noticed. He was busy, instead, taking all the credit for Alisdair's decision that something must be done. She lay listening, trying to split a hair that she had picked from her head, exactly like the Grizels and the Maggies and the wife he so often said he wanted. He was rather shocked by her lack of reaction and grew more eloquent in her cause which he said he was now married to, irrevocably. The other word he used to describe the action that he and Alisdair now meant to take was 'irre-

108

versible'. He said he fully realised the dangers: once Sarson was bearded on the subject, there could be no return to the present situation. But he and Alisdair had definitely decided to blow things wide open. He said it all ten times and she lay there nodding in agreement. Then he stopped pacing round the room and sat at the bottom of the bed and shook her feet.

'You understand what I'm saying? . . . I've *engaged*. I've decided at long last which lobby door is for me. And it means, apart from anything else, that I won't have to be jealous and resentful of your certainty any more. It always made me feel guilty and inadequate.'

She nodded. She said, 'I think it's fine, dear heart. But don't go it alone. No heroics. Stick with Alisdair.' Then she asked, 'You're sure Sarson didn't pay you off in some way?'

He shook his head. He said, 'Of course he's been kind in the past. But he's got nothing on us.'

She took no more steps to dissuade him. She seemed, contrarily, totally disengaged, even uninterested.

'You're sleepy,' he said.

This was one of the worst asthmatic attacks of her life. She was still buffeted by it in the middle morning when the sun began to shine through the bedroom window. The noises of the suburb were more cheerful than usual: the loud knock at the neighbour's door, the greengrocer's boy and the milkman rattling crates of empty bottles. It was quite a different sort of noise from Glasgow. In Kelvingrove there had been the trams winding up to rush the little hill ringing their double bell; a steady hum, with cackles and low gossip occasionally floating up to the window and people always asking after Stella. How's Stella? Stella to be proud of.

She lay now, naked from the waist down, half-covered, part-stunned, desirable and done and warm; not merely like a prostitute; but like a successful one.

Oh, you big one, Stella Vass.

Chapter 10

Miss Parker, Sarson's secretary, was a creature of the old building. Her beads, tweed skirts and bicycling blouses went with dark corridors, partners' rooms, linoleum, copper-plate writing and polished brass.

'In the *war* . . .' she used to say whenever a situation grew prickly – and with Miss Parker, somehow, most situations did. She was no less strange than any other middle-aged spinster. When she was not correcting junior secretaries for their manners or business in-efficiency she was inclined to tell them about her more hair-raising sexual experiences which were rum, rum indeed.

'There is already a visitor for J.T.S.,' she told Andrew as soon as he arrived in his office. 'But I've coped. He's in Visitors A.'

'What does he want?'

'To see Sarson, of course,' she replied with a scream of laughter. She treated all the young men as if they were fools, except at the office Christmas party when she approached them in an altogether different way. That always ended in tears.

The visitor turned out to be very important. Anonymous and commuting, he was one of the most eminent members of his profession, but solicitors take a pride and a slightly unhealthy pleasure in hiding their light. He was an old friend of the Sarson family but he did little work for the bank, nowadays. He was employed predominantly on government affairs. In Visitors A, the

V.I.P.'s waiting-room which had all the worst, padded features of a self-indulgent executive's suite, he avoided stating his business, but, upstairs, Sarson reacted seriously to the surprise call. He told Andrew to wheel him in at once.

Andrew had no chance to speak to Alisdair privately, but they had both observed the look on Sarson's face. It excited Andrew. It seemed to be evidence of his guilt. If anybody in higher circles had come to the same conclusion that he and Alisdair had done, in Glasgow, then it was more than likely that a solicitor would make the first tentative enquiries. But by the time the solicitor arrived in Sarson's office, the chairman had recovered his *sang-froid*.

'Teddy,' his voice was as lazy as a guardee's. 'You should have rung. We'd have come round to see you.' Sarson was an experienced negotiator. He did not ask the solicitor what his business might be. The implication was that he already knew, and was not afraid. The misunderstanding, whatever it was, would soon be cleared up.

Sarson introduced his son-in-law and the solicitor shook Alisdair firmly by the hand; one big, violent shake.

'How-do-you-do, Mr Pitt,' on the same, low note. Then he turned back to Sarson, while Andrew hung up his coat.

'You look disgustingly healthy,' he said, eyeing him more like a doctor than a lawyer, but the same could not be said for himself. He had a face like heavily creased parchment, varying in colour from the darkest grey to a sort of yellow Devonshire cream. He looked as if he had been sixty-three for a hundred years. He had big black, almost Italian eyes and the pouches of skin beneath them gave him the look of a sad, sad blood-hound. He was tall, but with a bad stoop. He wore boots, not shoes.

Offering him a cigarette, Sarson said gently, 'You look about as sick as usual,' and Andrew brought up a chair.

In spite of the excitement in his eyes, Sarson's voice was lazier, now. 'Somebody said you'd bought a boat?'

The solicitor nodded, then let his chin sink back into the stiff white collar. His stud showed above the knot of his tie. 'For my children,' he said.

'How big?'

The solicitor looked carefully at Sarson, much as if he were about to sentence him to death, then replied, with a sigh, 'Sleep five. Nothing very grand. They keep it down at Christchurch. But that bloody, damn Portsmouth Road is too much for me. Myself, I never get further than my own front gate.' Slowly he turned and looked at Andrew. 'I'm a dull dog,' he said with a little chuckle that shook him, then the eyes switched, almost with a click, back to Sarson. 'I thought I'd have a word with you, Jakie.'

Sarson was sitting up straight. The danger seemed to exhilarate him. He looked very young and well. Little pink patches had formed along his high cheekbones. He nodded towards Andrew. 'You'd better meet Vass. He's my manager.'

The solicitor's eyelids were almost as heavy as armour. They clicked back as he took in the younger man, as if he had never seen him before. Then again very politely he stood up and shook him by the hand.

The solicitor's voice was low and lugubrious. Andrew said vaguely, 'We did meet downstairs.'

'It isn't exactly the hand of Judas,' the solicitor said, 'but I can't say I'm here to hand out prizes.' Then he looked back at Sarson. 'Should you and I have a little chat first –'

'No point,' Sarson said swiftly. 'These young men share the work with me. I've no secrets,' he added, still with cat's eyes.

'I see,' the solicitor replied, rather vaguely.

He sat down again slowly. He lowered himself the final inches gingerly, as if there were no flesh there at all: only flannel underfugs. Andrew glanced at Alisdair, who sat, looking in front of him, coolly. Andrew assumed the same expression. The interview began slowly. Pushing *The Times* to one side Sarson then said, 'I see Willie Draper's dead.'

The solicitor nodded. Sir William Draper had been an official of one of the law societies, a former Lord Mayor. 'I can't say I'm sorry.'

'He was all right.'

'He had an infuriating habit,' the solicitor replied slowly, 'of calling me Tommy, not Teddy. He did it at school. He did it at Oxford. He did it in the Temple and he did it in the Club. And I'm not sorry he can't do it again.'

They all smiled. Sarson, at last, looked up at the monstrosity of a modern clock that was fitted on the wall. 'You'd better fire ahead.'

The solicitor nodded. He looked carefully at both the

Chairman and the young men, each in turn, without haste. Then in a low serious voice, he began.

'Before everybody gets excited and starts serving writs and all the rest of it, I always think it's best to meet the other parties and simply ask them if they've got anything to say. There's no question of evidence here. Officially this meeting, usually the most important of the lot, simply doesn't exist. Now is that understood?'

Andrew nodded, violently as if suppressing excitement, like a child of ten. The Chairman leant back. He had grown a little paler. He pulled the skin tight over his nose and stroked the bridge of it.

Alisdair then asked, tentatively, 'Are you representing a German firm here or –'

The solicitor raised his hand. 'Let me say my piece, young man. It'll all come out.'

But Sarson, too, interrupted. 'One thing I do think ought to be clear, Teddy. Are you speaking to me, or to all of us – to Sarsons Browne?'

The solicitor closed his eyes. Then again very slowly he said, 'That's one of the points I want to clear up.'

'This could be serious?'

'Certainly,' the solicitor replied, then added thoughtfully, 'Deadly.'

The Chairman spoke a little more arrogantly. He said, foolishly, 'It sounds like a bit of gossip to me but you'd better fire ahead.'

The solicitor could be acidly tough. 'I wouldn't be here on a shred of gossip. It's factual enough.' His next remark puzzled the Chairman and took the young men greatly by surprise. They both looked stiffly in front of them, with bright eyes, when the solicitor said, 'I'm

115

representing, more or less, a worried bloke who has just had a long talk with somebody who has been staying in a hotel in Glasgow.'

He turned his eyes sadly on to the two young men, both of whom now began to blush. The Chairman was puzzled and surprised but he did not ask the first question which came into his head.

He said, 'Who stayed at this hotel?'

'In fact, a shipping man.'

'We don't do any shipping business.'

'You don't know the bloke. . . . You haven't lost anything there. He's a pompous little Glaswegian upstart with a long watch chain and a high opinion of his own abilities. But in this case it cannot be denied that he has acted like a responsible citizen, even if you or I might have gone about things in a different way.'

'Must we be so bloody roundabout?' Sarson asked sharply.

'I beg your pardon?'

'You're being infuriatingly enigmatic.'

'I am trained to be infuriatingly enigmatic,' the solicitor replied. Then almost in the same breath, he went on, 'These two young men of yours seem to have been up and about early on Monday morning discussing at the top of their voices the revaluation of the Deutschmark.'

Sarson reacted swiftly. 'They had every reason to do so. We have just made a pile on a swap.'

The solicitor nodded and they all took it in. It was Sarson at his best: the old boy net in the 'swap' language, the ambiguity in his pleasant, cheerful smile, but nothing said which could not be taken to mean that the profit was natural, moral, unexpected and damned lucky.

Looking at his big bony hands the solicitor said quietly, 'In which case that part of the conversation has been recorded accurately,' and there was a clammy little silence. The solicitor again turned his big, sad eyes on the young men. 'I gather this conversation continued that night after dinner in the hotel. I believe it was in an upstairs lounge, deserted except for you and a couple of other parties one of which included this ageing ship-owner with the big ears? I speak metaphorically.'

Andrew and Alisdair sat quite still, not looking at each other, believing they were admitting to nothing. But Andrew's guilt would have been obvious to a bone-nerved window-cleaner ten yards off. He looked bright-eyed and younger every moment. The solicitor droned on:

'The situation, from the lawyer's point of view, is an intriguing one. It is reminiscent of another case going through chambers at the present time.' He spoke on the point, levelly, but as if he had all day to spend with them. The very tone of his voice and slowness of his movements seemed to be a threat to Sarson: here was the sheriff talking – don't try and hurry him.

'In this other case the following situation has arisen. A gentleman serving time for manslaughter was referred to in a magazine with a careless editor, it would seem, as a murderer. From prison, he is suing. The defence is fair comment. To establish fair comment they have to prove the plaintiff was guilty of murder. To do this they will have to re-try the murder case.' He sighed. 'I wonder if I make myself clear. In other words, to decide libel this jury will have to decide who was guilty of murder in the first place. If they decide the plaintiff was, he will lose his case, that is all. He will continue his stretch for manslaughter. The law is as just and as boss-eyed as that.'

He paused, and made a verbal paragraph as only an elderly man can do, taking his time and at last lighting his cigarette which he had held unlit in his fingers until this point. He cleared his throat and continued. 'Intriguing from the legal point of view. Coming to our case, which I would suggest is a little more important if less dramatic than murder,' and he paused as Sarson took the warning, 'We have similar complications. Allegedly. Allegedly. . . . Allegedly two young men sit around a Glasgow hotel saying, as I see it, the following things. One, "Our Chairman told us not to exchange some Marks into pounds on Friday when on our programme we were due to do so." Two, "Our Chairman went to a meeting of the Directors of the Bank of England at lunch time on Friday." Three, "Our Chairman by delaying the currency transfer has made our Bank over half a million pounds." Four, "We believe our Chairman made us delay the exchange only because he had some special knowledge." Next, "We will go and beard our Chairman on this point." Next, "If we don't gain satisfaction we will see other senior partners." Last, "If we still do not gain satisfaction we will take our case to the editor of the *Financial Times* and other serious and responsible citizens connected with the City."' The solicitor stopped and nodded. He said slowly, as if emerging from other drowsier thoughts, 'I speak from memory.'

The young men still had not moved and did not dare

to now. Andrew ocasionally glanced at his friend's face, then stiffly in front of him, again. Out of the corners of their eyes they could both see the statue behind the desk. Sarson had become stone. To these immobile people, however, the old solicitor continued to talk. He did not seem to be impressed by their reaction or affected by the dead silence.

'If this comes to court, true or untrue, let me remind you that it will take the front page every day for a week. In City newspapers it would displace the dropping of an atom bomb, and there are some complications I have not yet mentioned. On the other hand, I wouldn't be here if I thought it was going to get that far. In fact, I don't see why any action of this sort ever gets to court. Except that most people have greedy and incompetent lawyers. There's nothing settled in court that could not be settled at half the price, outside.'

Alisdair at last broke in. He said loudly, unsteadily, but with a sudden, splendid flush of courage, 'Unless, of course, one of the parties would like the case to be tried in public.' And Andrew, stupidly, violently nodded in agreement.

The lawyer dropped his head as if Alisdair had suddenly said or even done something embarrassing, like open his fly buttons. He evidently decided, in the end, to ignore him.

He said, 'I have not yet explained all the aspects of the case. The two young men in the hotel ' – and he slipped in a hard dig against Alisdair here, again as token of warning – 'who were obviously silly in that they did not want to be overheard, but were overheard not once but twice – were overheard, as I say, by a complacent enough ship-owner who returned to London and spoke, without being overheard, to a director of another merchant bank who is also a director of the Bank of England. This gentleman acted with rapidity and resolution. He is at present acting, or rather instructing me to act against my advice.'

They all listened intently. At the mention of the other director Sarson had leant forward. The creak of his chair startled Andrew. They were obviously all trying to work out who it was, who lately, had done any shipping re-organisation or new issues? The solicitor, as good with an audience as a top parliamentarian, gave them just time enough to guess for themselves that it was a very important man, indeed, but he did not divulge the name. Then he continued:

'This man wants me to sue the young men concerned for high damages, his case running as follows. As a member of the Court of the Bank and the sub-committee concerned with foreign currencies –' for a second he was interrupted. The Chairman sat back rather noisily and snapped his drawer shut. Surprisingly, he was smiling.

' I am sorry, Teddy, continue.' He spoke as if he were himself in no way involved in all this but had been called in purely for objective advice. Beside him the two young men looked pale, frightened and spiteful.

So the lawyer went on, ' As these things go, my client feels he has been damaged, in that the young men have attacked the honesty of the workings of an organisation for which he is partially responsible. He would know of the other Chairman's foreknowledge. He would also be in a position to know when the other Chairman's bank

bought or collected a large number of Marks. Such trans-
actions evidently come to the notice of Threadneedle
Street and require their permission.'

The lawyer sniffed and sat back, putting one hand
behind his chair.

'I don't think it's too solid a case,' he said mildly.
'We might get away with it. You can take it that I'd
have a good try. But fundamentally, everybody knows,
you can't damage an institution. The Board or Court
can't sue and in a way it's them, not any single director,
who suffer loss of reputation from this kind of rash
attack.'

He tipped forward suddenly, almost like a dummy,
doubled up; a man shot in the stomach. He opened the
cigarette box and took another cigarette. 'Anybody been
to a bone-pusher?' he asked.

Everybody said, 'Yes.'

'You might be so good as to write his name down. My
spine's in the shape of a U.'

They all stirred, but still avoided each others' eyes
until the solicitor called their attention again with a
loud, 'Well, Well. . . . What we're interested in is why
this gentleman, in spite of my gloomy warnings, instructs
me to pursue the case. Could it be that he has a personal
vendetta running with the young men –'

'Or their Chairman,' Alisdair suggested.

'Or their Chairman,' the lawyer agreed. 'That's true,
but it's a risky, roundabout way of attacking him. Surely
it would be better to leave the young men to do
that?'

'He might believe that the young men would lose their
courage,' Alisdair said firmly, his voice like a strong,

single thread. He looked white. But his brain was working. Andrew, on the other hand seemed to be dazed; even inattentive, now.

The lawyer sniffed. 'Another, subtler motive is the one that suggests itself to me. The gentleman smells mud. There is going to be a great deal flung around – libel case or Tribunal – and the sooner therefore he gets his own word in, saying, "I am nothing to do with all this," the better it is for him.'

'Exactly!' Alisdair agreed, emphatically. 'That's precisely how I see it. And I'll bet that's how it is.' And now for the first time he looked up at his father-in-law who was at that moment smiling thoughtfully to himself, still apparently quite detached from the scene. Then, as if uncurling, Sarson moved and spoke. His voice was like the sound of cool, distant water.

'There could be one other explanation.'

He rose from his chair behind the desk and walked to the double window, squinting down at the traffic below. The others waited.

Sarson did not use the third person or bother with any of the lawyer's qualifying adverbs – the 'allegedlys'. He said, 'This other chap, bless him, might be coming to my rescue.'

'How's that?'

It was the lawyer who asked the question, but Sarson answered Alisdair. 'It's just possible, you know, that I am an honest man. Also possible that he, another honest man, sees that beset by disloyal assistants I am going to be put in a fairly tight spot. He therefore uses his brain, again bless him, whoever he is, and starts proceedings, or threatens to, because he knows, first, that I can't be harmed by them but, second, that only a stinker would bother to take his son-in-law to court on slander. He's therefore taking action on my behalf for the protection of my name. I like the sound of him.'

As he spoke he switched on the box on his desk. Miss Parker answered huskily, 'Yes?'

Sarson said, 'Bring me a list of members of the Court of the Bank of England,' without a 'please'; and as he did so, there was an odd noise in the room like a stifled sneeze. They all looked up at Andrew, whose face suddenly was wet with tears. He did not hide it, but looked about him in a puzzled way, as if the tears and the strange little sob had been planted on him. Then they looked away again. Alisdair's expression grew harder. Sarson himself did not speak until Miss Parker had brought the list.

'Good,' he said to her, and taking in the scene, with excitement, she billowed out of the room again, beads clattering. All Wimbledon would hear of this.

Sarson sniffed and looked down the list. Then he handed it to Alisdair who took it, mystified. Back at the window, for an instant, pushed against the pane, Sarson said quietly, 'I don't suppose I have ever heard of a more slippery little plot, the motive for which, we can see written straight across my manager's wet face, was personal gain. I assume you would have put some sort of brace on me in order to blackmail me and you would have been disappointed, but my colleague – whoever he is on that list – is right in thinking that I wouldn't have done much more than bawl you out. This would have been damaging. The Glasgow ship-owner, one assumes, would have gone away with a pretty funny idea of how I work, and how the Court does. My colleagues on that list would indirectly have suffered. . . . Now if I were to ring up one of them and say "What did we talk about on Friday at lunch?" you might suspect collusion. You, Alisdair, will therefore choose any single director and we will call him here, in front of Teddy, and you, both of you, and we will put to him the question of what we talked about on Friday.'

'If that's so, we'll –' Alisdair started, with a frown, but Sarson interrupted. He spoke with a curious, swift harshness.

'You must learn, Alisdair, in delicate situations, never to anticipate actions out loud. Events in a conference twist and turn. Never say what you *will* do. You may lose advantage that way.' He suddenly turned on Andrew and said, 'Do you want to stay, or be excused?'

Meekly and quickly, 'I'll stay, sir.'

Sarson turned away. Andrew took a deep breath and gave a funny little smile as if everybody would praise his courage. He mopped up his tears with a white handkerchief, took a cigarette which the lawyer offered him, then Alisdair chose a name.

'Thank you,' Sarson said, and rang him up. Alisdair had conveniently chosen one of the directors from a large bank close by, not a close friend of Sarson's and one of similar standing and weight. He was, in fact, known for his military air: his voice had something of the Sandhurst clip. His Brigade tie was part of him. He was, of course, an Alexander man – for Monty, he had a patronising smile.

On the 'phone, Sarson said simply, 'My integrity has been questioned in connection with my activities in

Threadneedle Street by some people here in my office. I would be much obliged if you'd come round.'

They all heard the voice say, 'At once.' Andrew's reaction was again alarming and embarrassing. He gave a funny little choke as if he were about to laugh, yet tears came to his eyes again as he suppressed a smile. The swiftness of the other director's reaction, the kind of royal alliance that existed between these great barons had excited and affected him suddenly like the Trooping of the Colour, the sight of Winston Churchill or a flourish of Herald's trumpet in *Henry V*.

Then coffee was brought in. The lawyer was quite unmoved, so it seemed, by the drama round about. He asked Sarson, 'You got a boat?'

'Yes.'

'Down at Cowes?'

Sarson nodded. The lawyer took four spoonfuls of sugar, with a leer. 'Do you get down there often, then?'

'No, bloody seldom,' Sarson said. 'It's hard enough getting home. Two or three times a year at most.'

'It's a good sport, I think,' the solicitor said with his usual solemnity. 'You can go on at it even when you're more or less decrepit, always provided you don't fall over the side into the sea. . . . That bastard Willie Draper used to be a big noise at Cowes, didn't he?'

'He used to make a big noise,' the Chairman corrected, and the solicitor gave a dry laugh, almost a giggle.

He then said loudly, 'I'm glad he kicked it before me, else he probably would have written one of these "W.D. writes" obituary notes in *The Times* . . . "I knew Tommy for forty years or more," he'd say . . . "Tommy"!' Again he laughed loudly, with a dry cracking sound in his throat, then sat drinking his coffee, chuckling more softly to himself about Draper. A moments later he asked, abruptly, 'He was a Jew-boy, wasn't he?'

'I don't think so.'

'Oh well, maybe he was a Scot. He was an ugly bastard, anyway. I don't know whether he looked worse with that carrot thatch or when he'd a nut like an egg. He was short in the leg, you know. Duck's disease, like a woman. And fat in the arse. Poor old Willie Draper . . . he couldn't drink,' he added.

Chapter 11

None of them left the room during the break which dragged on for almost half an hour before the witness freed himself from a Board Meeting in his own office.

Andrew's tears had dried up. Once or twice he even spoke up, about the dirt in the trains, and the way that Glasgow had not changed. Neither of his remarks were taken up. They hung about in mid-air, then at last painfully died away. But he seemed incapable of embarrassment now. If Sarson had not interrupted to talk to the solicitor, he would have embarked on a third embarrassing, unanswerable and irrelevant statement, like a boring child at a grown-ups' party. He seemed to be incapable of thought, so amazed at what he had walked into that he could no longer cope at all, but simply look on in impotent dismay. At least Alisdair, biting his nail, was doing his best to think; to recover from Sarson's surprising turning of the tables and to prepare himself for the next phase. Andrew, on the other hand, behaved more as if he were preparing himself for death, with a kind of hysterical resignation; a windy acceptance.

The next phase was brilliantly quick and to the point. There were no lengthy explanations, no pomposities. Information was exchanged in telegraphic form, the cryptic language of the less self-conscious millionaires. That Sarson and his neighbour could twig each other so swiftly in a complicated situation like this and not be tempted to stray from the point, suggested that the conferences in Threadneedle Street must go at ten times the speed of similar meetings elsewhere.

Teddy, there to see fair play, put the questions, simply, to the witness.

'Without going into details can you tell us what was discussed in Threadneedle Street on Friday?'

The witness paused. He was sitting in an upright chair that looked too small for him, also leaning right forward, with an elbow on his knee, in a rather operational, military manner. He thought for a few seconds and then answered very clearly, 'Yes, I can. Nothing of very great importance because there weren't too many of us there.'

The voice was light, as he remembered the agenda. 'One, an administrative thing as to when we were all going to fit in holidays, all that – who was going to hold the Governor's hand in August? Hols, in other words. Two, Fort Knox and the drain on American gold. Should we say anything? Mr Kennedy likes interest rates to be low so the Yanks keep lending and investing over here – all right in itself, but it can get out of hand and upset the boat. Three, what we've discussed every day since last Derby Day I should think. Common Market. This time, Sarson there flaying the gentlemen in Downing Street, in their absence, saying they were too secretive.' He gave a brief laugh. 'Four, though I can't think it's relevant – also Jakie talking – all this fuss about the Tweed, poaching rules, catching salmon in the sea, do salmon feed upstream, all the old stuff. Prompting this discussion, cold salmon and cucumber.'

The lawyer smiled. 'You don't do yourself badly,' he

said. 'Now, you've got to be sure you didn't discuss anything else of a financial nature?'

'Sure.'

'Did you break up into groups? Talk separately?'

'Naturally, it's only the Governor's do. Not the Queen.'

'Who was Sarson sitting next to?'

'As a matter of fact, me on one side, Bunty on the other. He came in about last, with Bunty. There weren't more than half a dozen of us, all told.'

The solicitor nodded. 'Are either of you on any sub-committee?'

'In Threadneedle Street?'

'Yes. You or Bunty, I mean, on any meeting which Sarson isn't on himself?'

Again the neighbouring director paused. 'None. But I don't get the point of your question.'

'It has one,' the lawyer said and then asked, 'In discussing the Common Market, did any single country come in for special treatment?'

'Yes. In a way – well, we talked about Spain trying to muscle in. I said I thought they'd got a neck.'

The lawyer said, 'Fine, that's Friday. Were you in any other days last week?'

'Yes, Wednesday and Tuesday.'

'Sarson there?'

'Lot of us in on Wednesday. . . . I think he was there.'

'Were any currency changes discussed at any time?'

'Ah,' the neighbouring director said. 'I think I rumble. All this has something to do with the Deutschmark and your Glasgow Turbine romp.'

The lawyer said, 'It has.'

'We never discussed the Mark, if that's what the worry is. That sort of fact goes before the big white chief and the committee, but what we don't have to know we don't want to know. It leads to hullabaloos like this. But Jakie wasn't on that committee, nor was I. The Mark revaluation wasn't discussed at the larger table.'

'Would you be prepared to swear to that?'

'Well, of course I would.'

The witness had hardly left the room before the old lawyer walked across and took his heavy coat off the hanger. He said, 'You don't need to show me down.'

Sarson said, only, 'I am obliged to you, Teddy.'

The lawyer nodded. Putting his scarf round his neck, he added, 'I'm more or less honest,' then he shook hands with the other two who were standing by their chairs as if they were waiting for somebody to say grace: they had the same nervous, uncertain, near holy look. Sarson showed the solicitor to the door, closed it, then came back. He sat down while the other two, involuntarily, remained on the carpet, on their feet.

Sarson pushed his hair back and blinked two or three times. He spoke very quietly and swiftly to Alisdair first, but glanced at him only once. Thereafter he looked firmly in front of him, at his desk.

He said, 'You seem to have two alternatives. The first is that you are sued for slander by one of my colleagues and probably by myself. In which case you will not be invited on to the Board here. You are an ass and a disloyal ass, but I tend to think your motive was a fair one. Anyway, for the first time you moved on your own if only to shout about a Glasgow hotel that I'm first wicket down for the shits. If you take my advice you will go over to Teddy's, ask to see his client, withdraw every word of this nonsense you've dreamed up in some quite unnecessary mood of envy and vindictiveness; you will also discover the identity of this Glasgow ship-owner; you will give him a full explanation of your behaviour and a description of your error and of how before your eyes in this office, you were proved to be mistaken. This done your name will go up to my colleagues and we will cart you on to the Board, not as a bribe, but so we can keep a closer guard on your imagination, to which, as the saying goes, you are much indebted for your facts.'

'I am not sure I can accept that.'

But Sarson answered in the same cutting voice, 'Don't be wet at this stage, Alisdair.'

'I must think it over –'

Sarson rocked back. 'If you must.' He looked at his watch. 'You'd better write me a report on Glasgow, then go home. Let's hope Elizabeth has more loyalty. I won't say gratitude. I'm damned sure she's got more common-sense. Now go.'

'Yes, sir.' Alisdair hesitated, looked anxiously at Andrew and was clearly about to say something in his defence, but he was balked by Sarson saying again, 'Go!' fiercely, and at once he obeyed.

The door closed softly behind him. There was a little pause. Andrew was quite dry-eyed, but his face still looked blotchy; like a boy who has been bullied too much. He shifted his weight from one foot to the other and at last broke the silence. Even now, at this eleventh hour he was looking for praise, nothing else; for a reputation for doing the right thing in the end. He wanted this above all and not cynically. Black marks frightened him, still. The Colonel's son shone through.

He said with a feeble effort at a friendly smile, 'All I can do, I think, sir, is offer an unconditional apology for making a fool of myself and – and offer my resignation.'

'That won't be necessary,' Sarson said, picking some papers up from his desk. 'You've already got the boot.'

'Thank you, sir,' he said, foolishly and instinctively. Then he hurried out.

He wandered up to a pub in Mayfair and lunched there by himself, being excessively polite to the barman.

After that, he walked round the corner to a jeweller's shop where he saw two serpent bracelets in gold with many precious stones. He went in and asked their price and said he wanted to buy them for his girl-friend. He did not look shocked or surprised when they mentioned a price of over a thousand pounds. He looked seriously at the stones and said he thought they would suit her very well, for she was dark and tall. Then at last he dragged himself away, saying he would ring later, to confirm the sale. He left his own name, then wandered out and caught an empty bus. All the way home he imagined himself giving her, giving Stella – Stella Vesper and Stella Lucifer, Stella forever in ascendancy – giving her fabulous jewels.

Chapter 12

Perhaps we choose our friends with more art than we know. On one side of the Vass household was George, the bare symbol of integrity, but at the other was the crumbling, self-absorbed figure of Bill Williams. Again, there seems to be a Bill Williams in all our lives; the only married man we know who is more likely to fail than ourselves. He is therefore always closest at the times when we are at our most frail. Naturally, in spite of his charm, his generosity and his tragedy, Stella disliked him intensely. Like any wife, she was afraid that the neuroses were contagious. Any day which Andrew spent with Bill Williams was a bad one. But Bill materialised now, like a ghost with halitosis. He had cultivated rose-growers' side whiskers since his last spell in one of those hospitals where people go for sad short walks. He came fairly often, with a bottle and a bright and shaking smile, telling risky jokes about crack-up and crumbles and inventing a hundred schemes for making money. These visits prompted Stella to take a trip to a hotel by the sea about a week later, to find her cousin.

Neither the receptionists buried in their ledgers nor the waiters flitting about in the dining-room next door would acknowledge her existence, so she waited, stolidly, like a Caucasian refugee, until George walked in the front door.

'This is a very unfortunate coincidence,' he said

solemnly, walking straight to the bar, 'I had hoped to drink less today.'

She gave him a big warm smile and he grabbed her hand and pulled her on to one of the high stools.

'Morning service in this albergo,' he explained, 'is never of the best, but if you saw the nights here after the older residents have retired to bed, you would understand why.'

It was one of those bars that have an abundance of etcetera. There were little flags and a hundred little bottles; a strong smell of maraschino.

'What's yours?' George asked as he rang the push-bell which hid behind a box marked R.A.F. Benevolent Fund. 'And before you answer may I warn you that it's almost impossible to get a decent drink here? They prefer to make up lethal cocktails with onions, cherries, olives, crisps and a dash of bitters. The hotel is full to capacity.'

'You're hating it?'

'I am enjoying it enormously. I drink pretentious drinks, eat pretentious food in that Regency dining-room through there – this year renamed the *Restaurant du Soleil* – and after midnight here or at one of the jolly yachting or tennis clubs I meet pretentious little girls, all smooth and round and also maraschino, all hoping to become air hostesses. In the evenings we usually wear open shirts and gym shoes, but ties and jackets are required in the dining-room. The other bachelors here tell me that, outside Jersey, there is more maraschino here than anywhere in the western world.'

A South Coast girl, built for bungalows and dinghies and silver tankards, at last arrived to pour out the drinks.

She was in a white sweater and red trousers and she was young enough to be enjoying a hangover. Her conversation was entirely devoted to redescription of the party the previous evening. The girls had discovered, she said rather disturbingly, George's secret weapon. 'I mean his dancing,' she added, with hysterical gaiety, and literally doubled up with laughter, banging her head on a tap. Armed with Pimm's Number Ones, George and Stella then retired to the 'sun trap' which was a verandah with brilliantly painted straw chairs and a glass screen. It was very warm sitting there and it made Stella nod. She admitted she had not had much sleep since the Wednesday before when Andrew had got the sack.

'Bill Williams,' she described the subsequent days.

'Ah,' George said. 'In the house?'

'In the house, on the 'phone, in the air,' Stella said. In the sun she looked very white. The powder on her face had somehow formed a little drift by her nose. She leant her head back against the bricks and George, as usual, did not hurry her. At last, pitching forward again, she gave him a fuller description.

'Mainly, thank God, Bill's on the 'phone, but we've had one or two calls. They settle in together, like a couple of little boys, I suppose, only they don't play with Meccano any more. They just gas on at each other not merely building castles in the air but building whole, ludicrous futures – you know, they're going to open a restaurant one moment, or Bill's going to talk to some senior directors and see if they can bring Andrew on to their Board. . . . Oh, there's all sorts of plans, usually boiling down to "let's all go and spend a week on a motor launch on the Norfolk Broads and talk out the situation properly". Meantime, we've got about minus two hundred quid in the bank. It's funny, isn't it, how life can operate perfectly reasonably for years and then suddenly you're round the corner? Everything's in a complete shambles, yet there's more gin and tonics going down the throat and there's taxis and trunk calls and talk of expensive holidays; everybody smoking like chimneys, Elsa given extra money. *Deluge*, George. *La Deluge*, all of a sudden. If I don't get him a job, no one will. He's talking about it night and day, but he won't even lift the 'phone and make a serious enquiry. The most I got him to do was get the Oxford Appointments Board send him stuff and he goes through all their lists, with disgust over the breakfast coffee, saying how inefficient they are to send him jobs for which he's unsuited. It's odd, isn't it? The way things have changed. It's not love on the dole any more. I'd like to write a piece on unemployment, contemporary style.'

George shoved out his feet, scraping his heels. He said mockingly that he'd read it and criticise it, but meantime perhaps a synopsis would suffice.

'I'm serious,' she replied, as vaguely as before. 'It just pushes one farther away from reality, so it seems. Instead of living in a state of semi-disjunction, one's suddenly calmly whizzing round in outer space. He doesn't seem capable of being afraid, that's what's odd. He just won't accept it's happened to him and his reaction is curiously arrogant. He keeps on telling me to get the ice out of the fridge.'

George grinned at that. He said, 'Does he tell you he loves you or hates you?'

'That's complicated too, and maybe explains why I look like someone who has been waiting ten days in the Ladies' Room for the Siberian Express. He hasn't touched me. He's got every energy, so it seems, except the one that puts it in.'

'Does that offend you?'

'Yes. Well, he's not at his most charming, maybe, but –' she hesitated.

'You'd like the right of refusal?'

She frowned. 'That's not quite accurate, but it's maybe as near as we can get. I'd like the Siberian Express to arrive, you know what I mean? I've got a hunch that nothing will get sorted out while I lie on one side of the bed reading Agatha Christie and he lies on the other staring at the ceiling, like a corpse, until Bill Williams rings and the gins set in again. Occasionally he bursts out in a hymn of hate –'

'About Sarson?'

'No, never about Sarson. As you could guess if you used your brain. He hasn't yet summoned up the courage to say what Sarson is, although he knows fine what he's doing. He sees himself pretty clearly, every now and then. The only time he refers to Sarson is on the crest of the wave. "The best thing that could happen – a blessing in disguise. Bill absolutely agrees." We sometimes stick in that groove for about six hours, then the next one is, "I believe, underneath, that one of the reasons why I took a wild swing at Sarson was to finish the whole nightmare of the City, to opt out of a situation in which I was inadequate and disappointing the great pussy-cat. Father-figure stuff!" He'll say that once or twice really cheerfully. "The old father-figure stuff!

Good-bye last father! One must knock Dad! " You know how he goes on repeating things when he gets over-excited. Looking at the bubbles in the glass, he explains, " If your own old man goes early it's amazing how you go on picking up Daddies. That's the story of my life – but nevermore! Oh, no! Daddy's pushed me out and that's the best thing that could happen." Then he adds a revealing kind of rider. Cheerfully again he'll say, " And doubtless, in a year or two, we will again be best of friends. . . ." It's pathetic, isn't it, how we all go on? To know that much about the situation and still not be capable of helping yourself; that's serious for humanity.'

'Did Sarson lay you the other night?'

'What night was this, George?'

'The night to which I'm referring, Stella.'

She said, 'I know I'm blushing but it's not because the answer is yes. I thought you might ask me and I really couldn't tell you the answer. Not honestly. Not here.'

'Then where?'

'I could if I was in bed with you.'

George shook his head. 'You would not be in bed with me unless you had been to bed, before that, with some-body other than your husband.'

'Is that so?' she asked, absently, holding out her empty glass. 'You may be right. I've given up examin-ing Stella. I've got enough on my mind with Andrew.'

'They could be connected.'

'I don't know why I came all the way to talk to you, dear Cousin. I think you're being rather beastly. D'you like striking girls when they're down?'

'We're going to have to talk very carefully,' George

138

said, taking the glasses to have them refilled. 'Oh, very, very, carefully.'

'Are you feared I'll seduce you?'

'Yes.'

She nodded. 'Life's busting up,' she said. 'It's like that bouncing putty that bends, then bounces, then all of a sudden it gets thrown too hard and it shatters like glass.'

He looked at her very lugubriously, for a moment, then he said, 'In the yachting club there is a little girl called Belinda, who will be the age of consent on Monday next, and she's mad for me. I thought that would make a right climax to my holiday.' Then he went through to the bar.

He stood at the door with the glasses, when he came back from the bar, heading off a young bachelor who was interested in the new arrival, and Stella said, 'Now you're a spoil-sport, too,' but he did not heed her.

He said, 'You didn't really answer whether Andrew is hating or loving you, except to say he's not making love to you.'

'He doesn't know, himself. I can see why; I think it's encouraging. When he looks in from outer space and sees the crash and ruin ahead, he doesn't want to see me and the kids there too. So he does a funny thing. He treats us gently, like dolls, most of the time, saying, "poor, poor, lovelies", then he gets a bit drunker and still saying how much he loves me drops me a long story about seducing somebody else when I was giving birth to wee Jakie, only a couple of months ago.'

'Is it true?'

'Yes, I think it is. . . . I tell you life's getting very

weird. We sat there discussing his little chase-around quite calmly. Six months ago if I'd found out he put his hand on a girl I'd have walked out in a huff. And not satisfied with my reaction he goes on apologising about other girls too, saying he never got anything out of it, as if there were maybe a hundred. I asked him if he was trying to press me to leave because I wouldn't, and he absolutely denied it, saying that he only wanted the whole marriage on an absolutely honest basis.'

'What did you say to that?'

'Och, I lost patience around then, and told him not to be a bloody fool. . . . The hatred, what there is of it, is reserved for a more or less innocent character. Alisdair, his partner in crime.'

'He didn't get sacked.'

'Right. But oddly, Andrew doesn't even take a direct swing at him. Even there he hedges a bit. But he'll suddenly burst out about Alisdair going to church –' Quite abruptly she broke off and she looked straight at her cousin as if she were at the end of her tether. In an extraordinarily cold way she said, 'Unless we get a job for Andrew, it's all over.'

George had been looking down at his glass. He raised his head and seemed, for a second, shaken by the intensity of her appeal. 'About Alisdair at church.'

'Oh, that,' she said as if he had referred to a conversation they had had days before. 'Oh, he gets terribly worked up, and says that because Alisdair goes to church but doesn't actually believe in Christ's divinity he's not only wet, but a double-dealer, lining up with Judas. All nonsense, all logical.'

But a moment later they were surrounded by bachelors

with eyes pink from gin and swimming, and round tins of Senior Service cigarettes, all making maraschino references and B.O.A.C. jokes. Then girls materialised, all younger and rounder than Stella, all asking for more. They smoked and drank and talked about water ski-ing and late nights while next door the older residents, in heavy clothing, sat waiting for the *Déjeuner Cloche*.

The maraschinos persuaded her to come down to the beach in the afternoon. George insisted that he did not disapprove in spite of his glum look, but he certainly did not encourage her. It was difficult to judge whether she played rounders and drank more because she knew that George did not like it, or because she was only too willing to forget why she had come down to the seaside. An odd, unreal little drama obstinately developed. They insisted, the other boys and girls, that she should bathe and, not having a costume, she borrowed a pair of men's bathing trunks and tied a headscarf round her breasts. In the waves there were some coarse jokes, then when she came out one of the bachelors chased her to the bathing hut which they used. She almost let him kiss her, then with a laugh, and with the help of another girl, sent him packing. Oh, you big tart, Stella: Oh, you big one, Stella Vass.

When she reappeared, dressed, George had already started back to the hotel for tea. She shouted up the bank, but he did not turn round. The path to the hotel wound through dunes, up the bank, then past a wood which was the property of the War Department. What they stored there, or why it was necessary to put something secret so close to a perfect bathing beach remained unexplained. It was a hangover, everyone supposed, from some war, and nobody seriously objected. It had become part of the South Coast as the bombardment of Dover is part of the myth.

When at last she made up with George, she had a little quarrel with him, as if he were a stuffy elder brother, but he hated himself, it seemed, for taking up the attitude.

'What about your sixteen-year-old?' she asked. Then she grabbed his wrist and shook his arm and said, 'George, stop it: laugh. What does it matter? Why is all the maraschino forgiven, and if I try anything like it, you go glum?' He shook his head, but could find no logical reply. At last he said he was sorry and looked at her very sadly: she was tall and pale and blown about by the winds.

'You're my two-yard stick,' he said, and she stood very still for a moment, frowning. He explained, 'I mean, I've always judged other girls by you.' She walked on, suddenly disturbed.

'I've annoyed you,' he said.

'No.'

'Then why do you look like that?'

'Just for a minute there, you reminded me of Andrew.'

'Then Andrew loves you.'

'It would all be dead easy, dear Cousin, if he didn't.'

Bad-tempered children were going down to the beach avoiding barking dogs. It was difficult passing them on the narrow path back to the hotel and its bedrooms.

'Did you sleep with Sarson, Stella?'

She answered, correctly, with the lie. 'No, I didn't in the end.' He nodded, and again led the way, with long slow strides.

'If I had, would you make a pass?'

And he answered, correctly, 'No, why spoil a lovely, platonic, uncomplicated, sex-free, quarrel-free, brother and sister type relationship like ours?'

So she took his hand and they were friends again.

Chapter 13

Twenty-five pounds a week rising to thirty pounds a week is a governor wage. £1,250 rising to £1,500 isn't too bad a salary. Stella had absolutely no money grounds, therefore, for objecting to the job which George pushed Andrew's way. On this score she even deceived herself. Her objections, she told herself, were of a better, long-term kind. The job at 'the Fund', she said, could not possibly last, for the reason that Andrew was one of the least suitable young graduates in England to be employed in liaison with the universities. From Oxford he had picked up every habit and attitude which serious teachers elsewhere, as in Oxford, deplored. He had been one of the last in that post-war pre-Angry group of students, who had nothing to say for themselves and therefore lived a kind of Brideshead life with military overtones, absolutely unaware of the drift beneath them. His inaccuracies; his rash, spiral, synthetic psychological theories; the champagne touches; the charm itself were all quite ill-suited to the ruling academic climate of practicability, no nonsense, fair pay and Bitter.

She therefore went reluctantly to join him at his second interview with the Fund's European representative, Mr David Philbrook, who spent his life describing what the Fund was all about. Its headquarters were in a block of flats in Portland Place alongside luxury flats for knighted industrialists and doctors, American osteopaths and cake-eating Freudians.

The Fund's apartment was not large but it was tasteful and pastel, all grey and blue with a thick red carpet and a tall receptionist who also worked the telephone exchange. With or without spectacles shaped like Bambi's ears, she was instantly recognisable as an American girl; one of the kind who has refused to follow Hollywood and lose her identity in starlet's grooming, so looks like any other slightly unwashed New Yorker. With a show of many teeth and the faintest touch of Evangelism in her smile, she recognised Stella at once.

'Why, Mrs Vass, we've been waiting for you. Your husband said "a tall girl" but he didn't mention how pretty you were.' In the same soothing tone she switched through to the front office. 'Why, Mr Philbrook, we have Mrs Vass here. Shall she come right in?'

'Fine.'

'She'll come right in.'

'Thank you, Dorothy.'

'You're welcome.'

Voices like Muzak in the ear, almost breaking Stella's self-control. Philbrook's office was heavily camouflaged as an ante-room in an embassy, with flowers and beautiful things. She hated it on sight and as she was introduced to Philbrook judged immediately and correctly that he had already suffered the disillusionment which was bound to come Andrew's way. There had been criticism that the scholarships had been allotted in England on a rather narrow basis. The candidates both in the scientific and literary sections all seemed to have some connection with those more public dons, the ones who write for the Sunday papers, talk on television or in the bar of the Travellers' Club. A look at David Philbrook provided the reason. He was trim, good-looking and exceptionally well-laundered. It was gathered, in London, that he had 'lost' his wife. He was good at tennis and a regular church-goer (the Fund, after all, had Quaker origins); he read 'Religion' in *Time* magazine. He knew where to dine in Paris and he was a perfect skier. He never boasted any academic distinction himself. Indeed he was very modest, claiming only, in every syllable he uttered, that there was a right way of living, and he lived it. He was that sort of cosmopolitan, divorced, analysed Christian whose needle was set personally and professionally at Better Weather. He had the kind of guarded optimism that makes a man read what he wants into every letter and enables him to persuade himself rightly and completely into absolutely anything from racial segregation to yogi, but not into communism.

Andrew was sitting in one of those high, modern Jacobean sofas, the sides of which are held up with ornate gold cords. He looked pale, sober, almost convalescent and he was drinking a tiny glass of Tio Pepe. The job was already his if he wanted it. Philbrook looked at his Swiss watch. He had asked Stella to come down at short notice because he liked to meet a man's wife, and he was due, at eight, to take a plane to Karachi.

In spite of the shortness of time at their disposal both men put the position to Stella, Andrew gratefully and Philbrook generously.

'This is not exactly a charity, Mrs Vass, it is more like an Investment Trust, investing in men and women, and expecting no dividend. The capital remains the property of the trust, the dividends are society's. It seems to me your husband is a perfect man for this post: he has all the qualifications and if I may say so, exactly the manner we look for. If I didn't sound like an American,' he added with a laugh, 'I'd say educated yet positive.' He went on talking, but for a moment Stella's mind drifted away. She was thinking that if she saw this man in the first act, she'd cast him as a murderer. Philbrook, however, did not believe that he was projecting such a vivid image. He was confident that people trusted him. His voice, again like Muzak, was peculiarly easy to fade in and out, and when Stella drifted back to him he was finishing:

'. . . not a large salary.'

Andrew helped him out, 'Ah, but one doesn't come in to this sort of job in order to make a million. This isn't the Dick Whittington stakes.'

'Admittedly, Andy, but don't let's try and bluff Stella here, it is not a large salary. You will not become a rich man on it. But the trustees believe it to be a fair salary. It is more than two farthings,' he added, with a smile. His knowledge of the vernacular had the authenticity of the stalls seats at *My Fair Lady* both in Drury Lane and on Broadway.

Andrew went over the same ground, calmly and soberly saying, 'As you know, I've wanted to get out of the rat-race and here into my lap falls the perfect job: fair pay —' He paused again at this one, then looked straight across at Stella, 'Not champagne pay, as Dave says.' He paused with the complacent air of someone determined to keep down with the Joneses. 'But oranges and lemons pay, anyway; a little travel; fascinating people to deal with; a real sense of satisfaction.' He turned to Philbrook for help and got it.

'Absolutely. It's a most rewarding job in that way.

One is part of an organisation geared to help humanity along. Some of that rubs off,' he said with James Cagney's chiselled confidence.

Stella looked and felt like a big schoolgirl on the edge of a chair she was frightened of dirtying. She had not Andrew's chameleon's gift. She started asking unimportant questions in such a way that she seemed mean and small-minded. They joined together to answer her patiently. No, a scientist was not called for. At no time would Andrew have to judge a candidate's academic qualifications. He merely had to judge men. No, it was not an older man's job. The trustees particularly wanted the organisation to have a young feel to it. Sulkily she came round to saying that if Andrew thought it was right for him, then he had better snap it up. She refrained from saying, 'It sounds like easy money for some superannuated P.R. man.' But she was almost moved by Andrew's last appeal: not because he was impressing her with his arguments, but because he was so like himself again. The wool was pulled down right over his own eyes. In his mind was a kind of old Bourbon advertisement: silver-haired, in Washington, he was general manager of a huge organisation acting in a capitalistic world in preservation of older values. As he talked, he wrote the copy, and that is what made her shake her head and smile. He reached forward as he finished speaking and clasped her hand firmly. The gesture was impulsive. It almost at once reduced her to tears, in her exhaustion.

She turned away from him as he finished, 'This time no self-persuasion act. It's your sacrifice, mark you. We shall never be rich. Your sacrifice,' he added fairly, not for a moment realising that he was here speaking the truth. 'But I've no doubt about myself. It's miraculous, I think, how the job has come up at just this time.'

'I'm very happy it has,' Philbrook said. Stella stood up, snapped her handbag shut and quickly recovered herself. 'It's okay by me,' she said, then explained to Philbrook, 'I'm Scotch and we're cagey' – why, she wondered, do we talk nursery language to Americans? – 'That's just a fact. I hope you've not thought me rude. But Andrew's got to be sure.'

At the door Philbrook forgot her name and called her 'bride' instead. Feeling slightly sick, but at least in first-class surroundings, she paddled out of this suffocatingly charitable air, leaving the two men and Dorothy to fix the details. She offered Andrew no excuse. She had sometimes left places and parties like this when she was pregnant. Andrew always explained, after her abrupt departures, that she had gained a scholarship to Somerville.

Stella knew almost to the letter the report that David Philbrook would dictate to Dorothy and send confidentially to the Trustees in Washington. 'Something of an intellectual, a blue stocking with not too friendly a manner, I would say she was a liability in any ordinary commercial job and may indirectly account for Andy's withdrawal from City life. But in this job, she is a positive asset. Apart from her own outstanding academic qualifications she has the advantage of many friends in the provincial and older varsities.'

It started to rain and she went into the first cinema she saw. A nudist film was showing. The commentator reporting the asexual delights of this sort of community living had a smooth voice which she soon found indistinguishable from Philbrook's. Ten minutes after she sat down a man moved back from four rows in front. The cinema seemed to be almost empty. He sat down next to her, but neither touched her nor addressed a word to her. Once or twice she felt him look at her, goat like, in a rather startled, disapproving way.

Chapter 14

There were three empty rows at the back of the little lecture theatre in a downstairs room in King's College in the Strand when she reached there, three hours later. She took a place in one of these, unnoticed by most of the audience. But Alisdair saw her. He looked at her in a nervous but friendly way signalling for her to come across and join him, at the other side. Then seeing how wet she was, her coat, hair and particularly her shoes, he looked again, more anxiously. Continuing to smile uncertainly he left his friends and crept along the row to her. He stopped a couple of seats away, leaned across and asked, 'What on earth are you doing here?'

'It's open,' she said with real Glasgow hostility. 'Why shouldn't I come?' He shrugged. No reason why not.

'How did you hear of it?'

She said flatly, 'Sarson told me,' and Alisdair frowned. He did not follow that. She said, 'I didn't think I'd come but a man annoyed me in a cinema,' and she looked at him in the same flat, unfriendly way, again. Somebody in the row in front turned round as much as to say 'shut-up' and scotched Alisdair's next question.

'I'm soaking wet,' Stella said, quietly but not in a whisper, and several people, anxiously, went 'Sh sh!' 'It was pouring with rain outside,' she said. 'I walked.'

J. T. Sarson's talk on 'The role of the Central Bank' had already been applauded by the select but undistinguished audience and he was now answering questions, most of which were of that annoying kind asked by self-important people who already know the answers. It was a Study Group meeting of one of the Conservative Party's pressure clubs made up mainly of young managers, prospective candidates, a handful of journalists, a fascist or two and a large group of boys who worked in the City. These last, however, were not properly Kennedy-before-Cuba men, although they liked to think they were. They were too fond of their own voices and of Harold Macmillan's. Neither the study group, nor the pressure club itself, incidentally, had any power whatsoever, but the members liked to act as if they had. Occasionally they published some fighting articles on the danger of the Liberal Party, the old age of the Socialists or the Road Haulage Act of 1934. The group had all the hallmarks of an undergraduate society, but with a slightly lower average intelligence and higher average age.

Sarson had not referred to a note throughout his talk and he had spoken urbanely and slightly pompously, which exactly suited his audience. Confidently now, he answered all the questions as if they were sensible.

Stella spoke to Alisdair again, rather as if the meeting were not in progress; not noisily, with the intention of causing disturbance, but as if she simply did not acknowledge its existence. She said, 'Jennifer Sarson's a great hunting woman, isn't she?'

Alisdair nodded, more nervously, then put his finger to his lips and she looked at him as if he were feeble. Several people looked round at Stella as one of the boys on the platform sitting alongside Sarson now put to him a complicated question about the function and importance of the World Bank.

Stella (oddly enough, with a stupid look on her own face) asked, 'Is she a stupid woman?'

Alsidair shook his head. He said, 'We'll talk after,' but Stella did not seem to be in the least self-conscious.

'She doesn't come up to town much,' she commented and looking round behind her, lazily, she saw Salmon and another chauffeur sitting at the back. He bowed politely to her and she gave a loose half-wave, half-salute. Then she turned back to Alisdair and said, 'I've often seen photographs of her. A neat sort of face. She doesn't look as if she's got a grown-up daughter.'

Again Alisdair nodded and a young man who looked as if he sang tenor in the parish choir said, 'Please – it's damn rude.'

For a moment, then, Stella sat silently staring in front of her. The young man did not know the damage he had done. His face and voice, not his request, had aroused in her an anger as deep as it was illogical.

Oblivious to the danger in the back seat, the bespectacled group chairman, who was just under six foot six, now asked if anybody had any other questions to put to Mr Sarson, and without standing up, Stella said, 'I'd like to ask the speaker how long he thinks he's going to get away with it?'

Oddly, there was not, at once, any general sense of embarrassment, although Alisdair was already stiff with apprehension. He clasped his hands and stared at the toe of his shoe, practically disowning his neighbour. But some people in front, perhaps those of a more radical spirit, interpreted the question as pertinent if impudent.

One even gave a 'hear hear' and rocked forward in his seat, hugging himself and saying 'The voice of dissent.' Sarson sat quite still. He looked down towards Stella, recognised her, then slowly, even sleepily turned his head away again. Somebody shouted, 'Answer.'

'If the questioner would stand up,' the young chairman said, with a tolerant smile, 'we –'

As he searched for something witty to say, Stella stood up, unembarrassed and looked straight at the platform.

'Sarson?' she said.

He did not rise to his feet as he replied, 'I'm afraid I didn't hear the question.'

'How long are you going to get away with it?'

Sarson raised his eyebrows in an exaggerated way and looked at the group chairman. There was a ripple of uneasiness which increased as she said again, 'I'm asking you. How long are you going to get away with it?' Her accent was at its strongest.

The chairman of the group, altogether more anxiously this time, again rose to his feet. His chair scraped against the bare boards. There must have been sixty or seventy people in the room, all quiet now.

He said, 'Perhaps if the questioner could explain more fully what she means . . .'

'I'm asking Sarson how long he thinks he's going to get away with it.' Her voice was strong and steady. She stood upright and motionless.

Sarson shook his head and said to his neighbour, 'I'm afraid it's meaningless. . . .' He turned back to the boy at his other shoulder. 'Can you help us? What does she mean?'

'Sarson? How long are you going to get away with it?'

This time a small groaning noise went up from one section of the audience. The sort of noise that rises in a schoolroom when the boy who always asks questions, and only to draw attention to himself, asks yet another. But Stella did not seem to hear it.

The chairman said, 'I don't think there's anything to be gained by Mr Sarson trying to answer unintelligible questions.'

The murmuring died away. Everybody looked at Sarson who was staring straight at Stella, now, without recognition. Nothing could be read in his features. He seemed to be sitting for a dull portrait.

When yet again she said, 'Would the speaker answer me? How long are you going to get away with it?' somebody said 'poor girl' and a new murmur altogether more sympathetic, to someone mentally disturbed, rose then fell again. Reacting, the chairman of the group whispered in Sarson's ear. Everybody kept quiet, watching the platform. None of them dared look at the questioner.

'Answer me, Sarson,' Stella said in a slightly quieter voice.

At last Alisdair moved. What he said to her was inaudible but the drift was clear enough. He took her by the hand. She said loudly, once again, 'I want an answer,' then everybody turned round again as Alisdair, speaking softly and gently, said:

'We'll put it to him later. . . . We'll see him afterwards,' and things like that. Then he led her out of the hall. She went with him surprisingly willingly.

Some of the young officials who had so patently failed at the crisis now came out into the corridor too, and were anxious to put themselves right. At once a neighbouring room was commandeered. It was a small laboratory filled with jars and test-tubes and dishes and blackboards covered with equations, telephone numbers and reminders. Many people hopefully assumed that she was drunk. In this way they could more comfortably dismiss the incident. We know which we prefer, if we are offered the custody of an epileptic or an Irish drinker.

For a moment Stella sat quite still in an upright chair and said only that she was cold. Then she asked two questions about the room in which she found herself. Whose was it? What is a crystallographer? As they attempted to answer, she began to cry quite loudly. The noise of her sobbing considerably disturbed the little crowd which had gathered in the corridor outside. Alisdair said he would look after her and, not merely because he seemed to know her, the others returned to the lecture room where the meeting was now going with a buzz. A tea trolley was rolled in when the formal meeting broke up. It was there after every group meeting but tonight it looked as if it had been laid on to fight shock. Voices were pitched higher than usual. In the middle, Sarson calmly continued to answer questions about banking, denying that he and his friends could sack the occupant of Eleven Downing Street at will.

Next door Stella was recovering, too. She leant back her head and swung back on two legs of her chair. She pushed her fingers again and again through her wet hair. She was laughing a little now and swearing, easily, in a low voice, amazed at herself. 'Jesus,' she said, 'I didn't recognise myself there. That really must have been the Jimmy Maxton locked up inside. I never knew I could do that without a blush.'

Alisdair was too sympathetic; altogether too understanding, so inviting more trouble.

She said, 'Don't look so bloody tragic and sympathetic or I'll start the waterworks again, the "pity me". You're a bit of a puzzle, Alisdair.'

'I should think in your opinion I'm something worse than that.'

'Andrew doesn't love you very much.'

'I had gathered that. I've spoken to him on the 'phone once or twice.'

'Was he rude?'

'Well, not on the surface – the opposite.'

She gave a low laugh. 'For God's sake,' she said, 'that boy. . . . Do you know when he was a soldier he was a belt-of-honour cadet? He bluffed them all. Can you believe it? Or don't soldiers need moral courage? He just can't take a stand against anybody except, if he's drunk, against me.'

Alisdair was anxious not to get involved too deeply. He said carefully, 'In fact, I had hoped to get hold of you to see how he was but – well, I suppose wrongly, I accepted what he told me. That he had some sort of a Trust job. He was going for an interview. Was he offered the job?'

She answered, 'Yes.' Then seeing Alisdair's face she added coldly, 'Big sigh of relief.'

Alisdair was disturbed for a moment. Trying to keep

even keel, a little afraid of her now, he asked about the job. 'It's based in London?'

She never took her eyes off him. 'So I hear.'

'Not a big salary?'

'Not so bad. . . .'

'I'm glad. I'm sure it's the right sort of job. He's got such a personality.'

But Stella was beyond the polite stage. 'Which personality? You should have seen this week's programme. It would have made your ears burn. There hasn't been rage and repetition like it since the Venetian doge didn't invite his boy-friend to the Ball.'

But Alisdair again tried to play safe. 'You'll be staying on in the same house?'

'Oh, thanks, very much.'

'I'm sorry, I was asking a question. . . . I . . .'

'It was a damned silly question. Of course we are, unless Sarson buys us a new one just as a gesture,' she paused,' then added, 'for past services.' But Alisdair did not pick it up; or did not want to. He knew that she had helped Sarson on some matters concerning the Adult Education College and assumed – or at least, insisted on assuming – that her presence here this evening had some similar, innocent connection.

Stella looked round the little room, stretched out a finger and on the bench beside her wrote 'Dust'. She said, 'Funny how we always think of a laboratory as a hygienic crystal clean sort of place. How wrong can you be?' And before Alisdair could answer she went on swiftly in her special bantering, sarcastic way.

'Oh, dear me, no, we couldn't desert the suburb and Henrietta Barnet's last remains. You've no idea how I'm going to enjoy it now.' Alisdair was lost for a moment, and she broadened the irony, speaking with a kind of wildly sarcastic mock-bourgeois enthusiasm.

'No, really. I'm talking about our little grey home in North-West. It's what people come to London for. I didn't understand it before. It's splendid for privacy. You don't need to lift a hand for anybody else, and you can be perfectly certain that nobody will lift a hand for you. They don't interfere that way. Provided that you don't thieve spades or park your Vauxhall three or four inches too far to the left, you'll get left absolutely to yourself to have a good breakdown or whatever you want. There's no possibility of gossip. It's a splendid relief to us all.'

But Alisdair was too frightened and knew her too little to be sure. He eyed her solemnly. He said, 'I thought you didn't like it there?'

At once she replied, 'Oh, that was long ago when I had some curious idea that living's living, whatever the pain. That's why I used to object to the suburb. I used to give Andrew long lectures on vitality, the business of life being the business of bouncing off other people. But I've grown up since then. I don't retract, mind. Not really, but I've examined the premise, don't you see? Maybe energy's not an end in itself after all. I've been reading Zen Buddhism and all sorts. Since Andrew's assumed his Felix-went-on-walking act. He's what you'd call restless, if you wanted to be crude. . . . I'm getting very deep now, thinking bouncing's not maybe enough. So there you are, next to Stockholm the suburb's really your only European place. We'll get time to mature on our own. I wouldn't worry, Alisdair, these disasters are always blessings in disguise. That's what Mary said to her husband Darnley about the pox, the day before they blew him up sky-high.'

Alisdair nodded. It was all beyond him. He had never met women with feelings and forearms as broad as this.

'D'you know, when you open a boiled egg?' she asked him. And he nodded, half-embarrassed, half-afraid. The rims of her eyes were red. She said, 'Have you ever opened an egg and found nothing but a little dried up tissue and hot, smelly air inside?'

'No, I haven't.' Alisdair looked as worried as any curate. Stella sat back, looking bigger and older for a moment.

'Then you've never met my husband,' she said. Then softly, tears came back again. 'Open the window, dear, so we hear the cocks crow.'

About then, Sarson came in, and he took her by surprise. She expected him to come alone, in his greatcoat, stroking his nose, saying, 'Well, you certainly make a complete fool of yourself when you try.' Either that or not come at all.

But he came brilliantly with two or three committee members who looked completely flabbergasted as he stretched out both hands and said, 'Darling, I'm so sorry. I hoped you'd come.'

As more, different tears formed in her eyes, because there is nothing like courage to make one cry, she hated herself for not being able to shout out loud, 'Bastard! Smooth-tongued bastard!'

'And you certainly did come!' He laughed. 'These poor people aren't used to you. . . . What a curious place to put you,' he added, looking round the little lab. 'Gloomy.' Then he squeezed her hands tightly. 'You're feeling better?'

She said, at last, 'You amaze me, Sarson, so you do. . . .' Then she added, 'Alisdair's been very patient while I blithered on.'

He flashed his son-in-law a bright smile. 'How very kind.' Then touching her coat, he noticed how wet she was. 'But you're soaked, darling, kindness won't cure that.' He looked over his shoulder and asked imperially, 'I wonder if someone could tell Salmon to bring up the car?' He turned back to her, 'I'm afraid I won't be able to come at once. I promised these gentlemen another hour.' He raised his hands to stem their polite rejoinders. Then, at once, before she could object, he took her hand, raised her from the chair and introduced her as Mrs Stella Vass to them all, as the only woman he had ever met with both sex and a vote. She eyed them solemnly as she shook hands, hardly taking them in. But to all of them the couple suddenly had an extraordinary supernatural glamour, even grace. As Sarson took her out to the corridor, they all stood back and thought how they would remember the meeting. Sarson in their eyes was now twice the man. And they were particularly impressed by the way he implicitly trusted them. Turning back at the door like a star, exhausted after performance, she said good-bye to Alisdair, who gazed after her in blank amazement. Her pale face, the suède coat, the damp dark hair and long legs – these things impressed themselves forever on the memory of those who were there. On Alisdair too. A moment later she was huddled into the back of the Rolls and her knees and feet covered with a big fur rug.

But Sarson did not get into the car. With one hand on the door he stooped forward to make sure she was comfortable and wish her good-bye. The interior lights were on so they all saw him lean in and kiss her lightly. As the car drove off they saw her expression too, as she turned her face away, in confusion, and desperate excitement.

The journey proved to be a kind of cacophony of double disloyalties. Salmon was the surprise. They had not been going two minutes before he chuckled in a curious, low, clandestine way. He talked to her, as before, giving her due respect. But he said the most astounding things. First he repeated her catch phrase, 'Sarson, how long are you going to get away with it?'

She lowered the rug which she had pulled up to her chin and looked at the scrawny neck in front of her. The chuckle came again. It was a perverse, even a perverted laugh. 'Frabjous,' he said, 'I'll never forget it, Madam, never forget it. My friend and I, at the back of the hall, we could scarcely restrain ourselves. I would have cheered and cheered, Madam, but as you can imagine it would hardly have been in my interest to do so. "How long are you going to get away with it, Sarson?" The times I've asked myself that! The cry goes up, "how long, how long".'

He heaved a sigh. She sat looking at the driving mirror with big eyes. Now and then, as they passed some brighter lights, she could see one of his gimlet eyes. She said, 'I'm not sure I should encourage you to speak of your employer like that. You've got me in a fix here.'

'Nothing could stop me, Madam. I'm drunk tonight, drunk with the music of it. There won't be a chauffeur in the city doesn't hear of this. Your name shall be writ for evermore.'

Stella shifted uncomfortably. 'I could do without the publicity, Salmon.'

'Oh, Madam. . . . Do me a favour. I'm not cabbage green. It's not for me to divulge the private life of anyone who rides in his car. When I say your name shall be writ for evermore I do not mean literary. Oh, come, Madam. Do me a justice.'

She leaned forward, fascinated by the mental processes and restrictions, the mass of props, forces both pushing and pulling, which must work on a man for him to arrive at his sort of language in his sort of job. She said, 'I thought all you chauffeurs were true blues.'

Again the laugh came. 'That is our façade, Madam, purely our façade. For instance I know a very nice boy in the Life Guards who is a crypto-communist. You shouldn't be dazzled by our uniforms. . . . To tell you the absolute truth, Madam, you should see us meet together in the club of an evening, chauffeur-butlers. We have very nice exclusive premises even if the locale leaves a little to be desired. Not far from here, as a matter of fact, at the back of the Garrick Club, or put it another way between Moss Bross and St. Martin-in-the-Fields. There are many stars of stage and screen have *pieds-à-terres* in this district. You'd be quite surprised. You should see us there! Quite frankly, we're a witches' kitchen,' he laughed again his hollow conspiratorial,

May-day cackle. 'To be quite frank with you it gives me rather a secret thrill showing Lady Jennifer into the back of the car here, at election time. Cook goes down too, and I keep saying things like "I think we'll win the day. I'm confident, myself."'

He pulled up at some lights and talked now with more vigour. 'And on the front of the Rolls here, we have a bloody great huge enormous blue rosette and on the back, ever so discreet you know, like a C.D. sign, we have the name of the local Conservative candidate. I insist on that. Written up on the back of this beautiful Silver Cloud, you see, it only stirs up envy and class hatred. That little sign must gain more votes for the Left than any other between Oxford and Cirencester. I insist on it. And here, inside my pocket here –' he turned round and opened his jacket to expose a perfectly ordinary inside pocket, but he had the beady, ancient mariner's eye. Stella was leaning right forward by now. She looked at the ordinary inside pocket and gave a big child-like nod: a look of amazement.

'Right in there,' he said, and he turned forward as the lights changed to green. He released the handbrake and the huge car glided noiselessly forwards. He picked up the thread again. 'Right in there I carry two articles. They're next to my heart. They show my true gallup poll. I'm not a puny "Don't know" and I'm not a stinking Tory, no. I trust you implicitly, Madam,' he said as if 'implicitly' here could sensibly be emphasised as a refinement of 'absolutely', 'I trust you *implicitly* when I tell you these things.'

'I'm fascinated,' she said truthfully.

'Exhibit A. My red, red rosette. Vote Labour. I'm a

164

Labour vote. Born in Labour, bred in Labour, I shall die Labour, that's my aphorism. And beside it, exhibit B, as a matter of fact, I have a picture of the late Ernest Bevin stepping out of this car, giving me a kind thank you smile in spite of the appalling weight of responsibility on his broad shoulders at that time.'

And abruptly as he had begun, he now stopped talking. She said, 'That's very interesting. Ernie Bevin was a great man,' and sat back. He said nothing more on the subject until he had delivered her at the flat. She discovered with relief that he now had a flatlet of his own in the basement. He said it was adequate for his small needs. He switched on the electric fire and lights, poured her a whisky and soda, and laid out a bath towel for her. Then as he was about to leave he said, 'Sometimes, driving on my own I sing out, boldly, the chorus of some revolutionary songs. I'm not familiar with the verses. That makes me feel good. I don't think Mr Sarson will be long, Madam, and as I doubt if I'll be up again perhaps I may shake you by the hand.'

'Please. I'm glad someone was happy.' She smiled and shook his hand. He gripped it like a vice.

'Good lass,' he said, and vanished.

A moment later, the telephone rang and her reaction was first quick, then very slow. She picked it up at once and said, 'Hello.'

It was Andrew at the other end. He said, 'Hello, is Mr Sarson in?'

She replied, 'No, he's out.'

Then there was silence and very slowly they both replaced their receivers, as if they had seen snakes.

When Sarson came home, half an hour later, she was

still standing rather stiffly in front of the electric fire, in bare feet. He closed the door behind him and she did not say anything but remained hanging on to her tumbler of whisky with both hands as he unbuttoned her skirt. Then at last, she said, flatly, 'Hallelujah, I'm a cow –'

Chapter 15

'You know nothing about love and everything about sex.'

Sarson looked satisfied by her description of him. It was good for male vanity. But Stella meant it neither as a compliment nor as an insult. Simply as a fact. She felt dragged down to facts and facts alone. Her self-knowledge of which she was so proud seemed to have completely failed her. Like a motor-cyclist in a long skid she had, for three weeks, it seemed, been looking one way, pointing another and travelling in the third. Sarson, lying on his back, took up the whole bed. The hair on his chest did not grow levelly. She said, 'I think I like the look of you better when you lie on your stomach. Maybe it's that wound again. It gives you a kind of Alexandrine glory, Alexander the General, Alexander the Great. . . . People like you have to have fought a war, otherwise you're inexcusable.'

He said, 'Why on earth are you putting on your clothes?'

'Because I'm leaving.'

'It's only midnight.'

'I have a husband.'

'Oh, yes,' he said, huffily. 'Oh, yes indeed.'

'By the by, I'm leaving for good.'

'Don't be ridiculous. We're just beginning. You must admit it was bright of me to grab Salmon that downstairs flat. I knew you had qualms.'

She nodded. She thought to herself as she put on her

167

underclothes that she would never wear black stockings again. She sat on the end of the bed and looked at him. 'Glasgow' again, with that disillusioned look that makes a woman of twenty-five as old as she will ever get. 'You can afford absolutely anything, can't you? Has your wife got money, too?'

'A bit.'

'You wouldn't have a cigarette?'

'No.'

'Please.'

'There may be some in the chest of drawers in the sitting-room.'

'Thanks a million.' She wandered through. Her skirt was still on the carpet, in there, beside her shoes which were steaming in front of the electric fire. In the drawer she found packs of playing cards, boxes of writing paper, string, marbles, sealing wax, a snapshot album and a selection of paper knives, all smelling of 1937 – that drawing-room smell, cool and musty. She imagined Jennifer Sarson must smell the same, permanently in storage for a few weeks of summer. At last she found some cigarettes. She went back to Sarson whose eyes were closed.

She said, 'I'm interested in the money motive when you're already a strictly unostentatious millionaire.'

He sat up suddenly, this time almost imitating himself as a boy and said, 'D'you know it's time I had some hols? Dare I suggest a dirty week-end?'

'I'm not coming.'

'France, or maybe the Black Forest. That's fun, as early in the season as this.'

168

'To the woods,' she said, still without a smile, and he reached out to her. But she shook her head, sadly.

'You're wasting your time,' she said. 'I'm unwound and no one's going to wind me up again for quite a while. I've got to go and see whether it's possible to tell my husband a load of lies.'

He banged his pillow. 'I should think so. He's very keen on you. You can get away with a lot. I wonder why you married that one.'

She hit him hard across the face with the back of her hand and he lay back. His cheek was stinging but he did not raise a hand to it.

'Quite right,' he said, with a little sniff.

A moment later, she spoke again. 'If I wasn't bombed out, I'd tell you about conceit and cats. . . . Tell me, do you have run-arounds like this mainly to keep your mind off your work?'

He answered well, with a suspicion of a smile, 'Who said they kept my mind off my work?' and raised a hand lest she should strike him again. But she made no move to do so.

'I would have said it took a mind neatly organised into compartments to be able, without qualm, to sleep with a sacked assistant's wife and believe you can get away with it.'

'I'd still have made a pass at you, were you the Governor's wife.'

'Quicker, perhaps,' she said, and put on her slip. 'Your ambitions amaze me. But I think I'm getting there.' Then, in exactly the same tone she went on – 'Andrew rang here before you came in.'

He rode it well. 'Ah,' he said, '. . . you're lying, of course.' He sat up.

'No.'

Suddenly he looked furious. 'That's too much –'

'Oh, don't upset yourself, old man,' she said, picking a piece of fluff off his shoulder. 'He hasn't the money for a private detective. . . . I must have worked that out, at once.'

'But how did he know you were here?' He frowned, perhaps wondering if he had drifted into one of these 'modern-living' whirlpools, that drag people gently, in sight of everybody, to ruin, and have done so for a hundred years.

'He didn't know I was here.'

'Coincidence?'

'It doesn't follow.'

'Then why did he ring?'

'I fancy it's a mixed motive. Andrew's idea of strengthening character is to make yourself look somebody in the eye after he's done you a bad turn. That's one of the few things that come down from the Indian Army Papa. So now he's got a good job, or so he thinks, with a few dollars and more kudos, he is feeling strong again. I think he was ringing to tell you not to have him on your conscience, which shows (a) how much nicer he is than you and (b) what a dreadful cowardly wee boy he is, sucking up to the prefect even after he's been expelled. That's real insecurity. The other reason, a touch below the limbo-line, maybe, is that he can see from my face that I'm getting laid by somebody else and as you're the biggest ram in our round of acquaintances, he jumps, guesses and gets it right.'

Sarson said, 'He must have had some sort of clue.'

'Yes, he must.'

'Have you said anything to him? Done anything?'

'Not since we started. That's typical enough. The clues are always dropped before the act, I'm sure. Same as regret comes before action, these days, and apprehension afterwards. That's self knowledge for you. There's anticipation.'

'What sort of clue?' he asked.

'Inviting you to be godfather, that sort of thing.'

He lay back on one elbow and said, 'Oh . . . Gawd. . . .' with a smile. He was impressed with her sanity and looked a lot calmer. 'Will this mean pompous messages and talk of divorce?'

'If it does?'

'I'll have to pay him off, I suppose.' He blushed as soon as he had said it. She took a long time, staring down at him, before she answered:

'If you like to follow me to the bathroom you can hold my head while I'm sick. . . . You're a zombie, Sarson, a nine-life, no-life cat. My husband, if I guess correctly, is lying on the sitting-room floor at home, sobbing his heart out. Maybe more. Maybe contemplating shooting himself and his children. I can see them all falling down the stairs, flapping, like dead birds toppling off a branch. That's how these things happen. And I sit here with all that understanding, frozen, kind of powerless to do anything about it, just because I'm common enough to get in the hands and go back to the hands of a big uncommunicative cat who knows more about sex than love. Tell me, why did you swing that Deutschmark thing?'

Sarson hesitated, then he put his hands behind his head. He said, quite freely, 'I made half a million. If anybody suffered it was a Hun. That's what mystifies me about all this. Alisdair taking up an absurdly moral, pompous point of view. The biggest loser was Herr Doktor Adenauer. No one else. And he can bloody well afford it.'

'And you did it to pip him?'

'No, for God's sake – I did it because that way I make half a million.'

She asked, frowning, 'Can you go further than that?' But the request only made him cover himself with the sheet and groan.

'I don't know what the hell you're talking about. This is some of your Viennese nonsense, I suppose.'

But she was digging in her toes.

'Can you explain more why you wanted to make half a million when you've already got – I don't know – say, ten million?'

'Oh, Stella, you must be getting weak in the head.'

'No, but try.'

'Oh, don't be so boring . . . if you play a game, for heaven's sake, do you have to ask yourself why you don't want to lose?'

Annoyingly, she seemed encouraged by his reply. She said, 'That's good. Tell me more. How much of that money comes to you personally?'

'None, of course, you know that. On the other hand if the bank makes a load of profit then we won't have to alter things and in the relay race your Leftish friends so wrongly despise, I'll have done my little bit and hand over to my son Paul. It's up to him what he does with

172

it but at least I won't have presided over the liquidation. And I'll have had enough pocket money to buy a few nice possessions.'

'That matters?'

'Of course it does,' he exploded, 'unless you've got a pretty silly view of life. Why not have a Rolls Royce? And if you can also have a nice estate, some cows or even paintings, and hand them over, bully for you. It's common sense.' More seriously, staring at the ceiling, he said, 'That sort of possession is a kind of symbol of survival without humiliation. That's fair enough Norman thinking. It's nice if the change-over from one generation to the next can be dignified for a couple of hundred years without all that "clogs to clogs" nonsense. Believe me, my darling, there's nothing screwy and complicated about my viewpoint or any other sensible banker's, maligned as we always are. Horse-sense is what we need, horse-sense is what we admire, and horse-sense is what we have. Enough, thank you, consistently, to keep off you with your hearts too big for your heads and all those liberal young men like Alisdair with guilty sociological consciences, Oxford accents and economic theorists' doubtful rules of thumb.'

He stopped, smiled quite broadly. 'Now are you satisfied? I suppose all the time I've been hankering after your tits, which really are rather good, you've been searching for my motives. What a waste of life!'

'You're too right,' she said. 'I see that now bright and clear. You haven't got a motive, dear lover – a motive's a dynamic thing. You've just got an attitude of mind.'

He did not like it. He groaned again and looked up at the ceiling and said, 'Sticks and stones, sticks and stones. . . . Stella, don't be a bore.'

'I won't any longer,' she said and went to the door. He did not move. In truth, he was sleepy and glad, rather, that she was going; why, he didn't enquire.

'I'll ring,' he said.

'Don't bother. . . . Tell me, did you remember that I was with you when you saw the man from the International Monetary Fund in the street.'

'Yes,' he replied and looked at her. He nodded slowly, 'Clever girl,' he said. 'That really surprises me.' He clearly spoke the truth and she gave a big, much happier smile.

'I'm glad it surprises,' she said. 'I thought for a nasty moment you might have worked that out before you came into me in the lab, tonight, not caring who saw. If you want to know – that impressed me. You've got guts sometimes, I admit.'

'You've got lovely guts,' he replied and quite resigned to her departure smiled the pussy smile and stretched out his big arms, inviting her to stoop and kiss him good-night. Had she gone then, it would not have been a final parting. But she stopped to say something; to pay him another compliment, in fact.

'There's something else you've got which I hate, but I suppose other people would admire. You can keep a secret.'

He looked surprised. 'I thought I'd been nothing but indiscreet all night.' He readjusted his pillow, banging it with his fist. 'Somebody once told me that the real value of official top secrets was that in divulging them you could get top girls.' He laughed his loud, Cowes laugh.

She said, 'You didn't tell me any secrets about the Deutschmarks,' and shook her head. 'I'd guessed that one before your solicitor called. I remembered that I.M.F. man. But you're discreet about Andrew. He told me he had an accident when I was in hospital.'

'How unwise of him.'

'And he had a girl. Did you know that?'

'What's the point of the question?'

'Oh, you big Tom. Beau Brummel's morals, you've got. We're all bucks together.'

He shook his head patiently at this outburst. Then he said, 'You've got it all wrong. You seem to think we're all as self-conscious as yourself. I don't have little rules about the grades of secrets I'm right or wrong to tell. But whether I'm laying you or merely meeting you biannually at office parties, I still don't think it's for me to tell you that your husband's taking out somebody else's wife – any more than it is your business to tell me that he's got the moral fibre of a hermaphrodite.'

The line was delivered without emphasis. That it was a cross-counter for the slap he had received earlier there was no shadow of doubt. But the effect was greater than he ever could have expected. It was as if he had struck her in the stomach with all his might. She missed a breath.

'Thank you, dear.' Then again, 'Thanks very much.'

'I'm sorry?'

'Oh you,' she shook her head and turned away. She was laughing in a gusty sort of way. A rush of violent reactions blocked her, and she knew at the same time that she was on the verge of an asthmatic attack. Her breathing was already out of control.

He said, still lying down, 'Well, isn't it true?' and collecting her things she made for the door, almost drunkenly, saying only, 'You fool.'

She began to run, not heeding his shouts from the bed, 'Darling, if he's too bloody, do ring. I mean it. . . .'

She slammed the flat door behind her. She should have sat down in the lift but she stood arched in the corner, leaning against the angle. She should have rested in one of the easy chairs in the hall with the thick red carpet, or on that black piano stool. But taking small steps like a virgin frightened on her way home she hurried into Grosvenor Square, and walking round it and round it and round it – Stella fashion – she forgot where she was altogether. A police car gliding by took a second look to check if she were perhaps a prostitute, but less charitably assumed she was a 'Ban the Bomb' girl of the weirdest sort. She was still muttering to herself. But the mutterings and the gasps soon became irrelevant; all the noises concerned the fight against asthmatic seizure.

Chapter 16

An hour or two later, she drove back to the suburb, by taxi, preparing her speeches and explanations for the ordeal that lay ahead. She fancied it would go better if she could first change into her nightie. She spoke to herself loudly enough for the cab-driver to believe that she was talking to him and he kept checking his speed, but when she instructed him to drive on he too began to mutter to himself, expressing in cabbies' terms cabbies' ignorance of all human behaviour. Stella told herself that she could stand anything Andrew might do or say – except his tears. If he started to cry she reckoned she would at once pack her case, catch the first train from the nearest station and get a factory job, in, say, Nottingham, or Leningrad. But it was to go very differently from how she expected.

She found all the doors locked and ground floor windows closed. The front door for which she had a key had been bolted within. There were no signs of life downstairs. She could get no answer from Andrew, although the lights in the bedroom facing the street were all blazing. As she fumbled round the back through the dustbins and the coke to try and force the larder window she fell and hurt herself. Then she returned to the front of the house which seemed even lighter. The curtains had been torn down. One of the mean windows had been swept open, and there on the sill, sat Andrew with a paint brush and pot of whitewash. She came on to the crazy-paving path that needed weeding, and looked up at him sulkily, licking the knuckles of the hand she had hurt. There was a dirty mark, from the coke, across one of her cheeks. Andrew's voice was well controlled. He spoke steadily, almost cheerfully.

'But soft,' he said, continuing to paint, 'what light through yonder window breaks?'

The subsequent performance, however, would have suited Shaw, not Shakespeare, it being Shaw who required only of his actors that they should stand six feet away from each other and speak the words loudly and clearly. The distance was greater, and the separation almost vertical, but the principle was observed in a weird, cold way. The neon street light robbed Stella of any colour. She talked flatly.

'Are you going to let me in or aren't you?'

'In the end.'

'I see. Should I go away again, then come back?'

'No, you should stay exactly where you are.'

She bit her lip and nodded.

'We'll wake all the neighbours.'

'That doesn't worry me. It leaves me cold.'

'Not so cold as I am. And my feet. . . . I'm soaked through.'

'With tears?'

'Yes, Andrew, partly with tears.'

Andrew nodded, put the brush back in the pot and shifted along the sill, an inch or two. She refused to ask him what he was doing and stood obstinately waiting.

'How long do I have to stay out here?'

'That depends.'

'Do you want me to shout out and wake all the neighbours and say that you suspect me of adultery?'

178

'I don't suspect.'

'All right, put it the other way. That I have made a fool of myself?'

Andrew said, 'It's funny, isn't it, how one's friends make pigs of themselves but we only make fools of ourselves?'

She shifted; tried a sad smile, as she looked up again. 'Look. Don't be silly, dear heart, you've made your point. I grant you. You're one up, here, and you've made it so we've got to talk and that's good. So now come down and let me in and we'll have a Scotch and behave like reasonable delinquents.'

'There's no Scotch.'

She sighed. He was painting one of the uprights now, very carefully and slowly.

'I can't quite make up my mind which end to start,' he said, then lowered the brush. '. . . At the point where Stella picks up Andrew in an Oxford pub, or Andrew bathed in tears in Sarson's office. . . . You'll observe that I'm beginning to wonder if the fact that I've acted in love for eight years does prove that I must be in love, after all. I think the fact that I've acted in love maybe only means that I've acted how you want me to act – which isn't right and natural.'

She said, 'There may well be truth in that, Andrew, but don't be silly, dear. . . . I can't talk properly here.'

He ignored that. 'As I laid down the receiver a couple of hours ago, guess what happened.'

'I can't guess.'

'I want you to try. Or better, just tell me how you pictured me, when you yourself cut the line.'

She said, 'I thought it would hurt you badly.'

'Convert into action, please.'

She sighed again; swept back her hair. 'Please let me in.'

'Well, what did you say to Sarson that you thought I would do? From the delay, I take it you didn't expect me to come round and knock him out?'

For a moment her eyes were downcast.

'He wasn't there when you rang. I was alone.'

'What did you think I would do?'

She moved forward to the mean border round the house and tried to readjust a meagre magnolia bush which hung its head. It would not be helped. She set a branch against the pebbled wall, but as soon as she stepped back, it slipped again.

She mumbled, then lifted her head to answer him at last: 'I thought you might cry.'

'Good. Where?'

'Have you been drinking?'

'Yes. And I'm sober. Indeed for once the description stone-cold sober would make sense. Where were you expecting me to cry? In the bathroom.'

'Don't be silly –'

But he was talking excitedly. 'And for my tears, your pillow or your dirty underclothes?'

'Don't shout, dear,' she said.

A light had gone on in a house opposite. Andrew waved across to it cheerfully. 'Good-evening,' he cried, but the light went out again. Then he looked down at her once more.

She said, 'Are you going to finish by throwing that paint over me?'

'No, Stella. Oh, no.' He stared down at her solemnly.

'You've got it wrong. I don't see this as comedy.' Then he returned to the painting. 'But you were describing. . . . Am I on the bed, or on the floor?'

'I don't know.'

'Let's make it quite clear. You're not coming inside until we've got all these things sorted out. I'm damned if I'm going to be persuaded, suffocated, unreasoned this time by clouds of Stella talk, and Stella breasts and Stella breath, all of which, I confess, I find too comforting.'

Again she lowered her head. He pursued the subject relentlessly: 'Tell me, have you ever made love to him in the afternoon and to me in the evening?'

She stood quite still.

He continued, 'Clearly yes. How close have we ever got: Hours? One hour? Maybe forty minutes?'

'I'm not going to stand here, if that's the value of what you've got to ask and say.'

'Well then, I'll ask more romantic questions. When I first took you out to dinner in Oxford, at that Vol-Au-Vent Castle, were you happy?'

'Yes.'

'But not in love?'

'Andrew –'

'When we went up to London all those years ago, and met Gavin and all the other good Chelsea Mansion Officers, class chums I had, who gave you drinks, then drove us – where?'

'To a night club.'

'Right. Did you enjoy that?'

'Oh, for heaven's sake –'

'Or did you really enjoy the train back when you told me how little purpose they all had, and how you couldn't live like that, and how I was one better than them, and went on and on, about these things, until we lay on opposite sides of the carriage all the way back from Didcot, cold? '

' I hated that.'

' So when, twenty-four hours later, I visited you in that ghastly room of yours, which I should have recognised as a foretaste of Leftish living and socially real things to come, you cried? '

' I don't know where the hell you think all this is getting us.'

' I'm merely reminding myself that I'm not so bad, after all. The record's better than I thought. I'm blowing my own trumpet from the ramparts, honey-baby, and for a little while longer, I'm going to continue to blow.' She paced away a little but he continued in a slightly louder voice, ' So we went to bed, that morning, in the Iffley Road.'

' Yes,' reluctantly.

' And you were very hurt and angry that I didn't force you to do any more than lie in my arms? '

' I was very glad.'

' And that I took you then, to Scotland, and married you? '

' I was very glad.'

' And then no longer merely held you in my arms.'

' I loved you.'

' And from then, while I bagged the Sarson's job, and gave notice to the tenants here, and brought you to these altogether sunnier digs, and let you belt off your socialism at altogether sunnier friends? '

' I loved you. Now please let me in.'

'Good. . . . Then the world changed,' he said, suddenly sad, 'the whole world changed. Was it having babies? Was it finding that the Alisdairs had real capital? Was it falling out of love? Why did I stop hearing you, and start listening? . . . I'll tell you why, in a moment,' he added suddenly, more cheerfully, and again took up the brush. Below, she sneezed.

'Bless you,' he said and went on painting for a while.

She wandered away, tried the french window at the back again, breaking a pane of glass. But she could not reach far enough in to move the lower bolt, and he had had the foresight to take the key out of the lock. It was impossible to force the double hold.

'The gay tinkle crash,' he said lightly, on her return, 'of the cuckold's house of glass.' She was shivering with cold. 'I have an instinct,' he said, 'to make you undress completely before you come inside, but I won't indulge it.'

She asked if she could have a cigarette, and he answered 'no', then went on, 'The peculiarly bitter thing is that I chose the underclothes, not the pillow, and I wept on the floor, not on the bed, expecting you to arrive within the hour to stifle my sorrow. But I didn't put on the heater and you gave me time to grow very cold. That's when I took against the wallpaper. Then you gave me time to think. And time to think why I had listened to you. And time to realise for the first time that I'm not, as you sometimes imply, merely a rather borderline boy, but that I'm a nice romantic, if pink-cheeked, Romeo and I have a great deal more in common with our neighbours hereabouts, than I had ever guessed. Indeed this little balcony demonstration is well thought out. I am for the first time relieving all of them by indicating publicly – I do wish there were more to hear – that I am not, after all, as I have so consistently pretended to them, to friends in the City, to other women I have encountered and dropped, to everybody, in fact – I am not after all a three-babied Romeo. I am not any more obliged to worship, uncritically, the beautiful circles of your mind, the purity of your intentions, the strength of your heart. Because in sustaining the romance, I have done as these other asses hereabouts have done, namely veered more and more towards your ideas, endeavouring more and more to satisfy your demands. In fact you have not been so simple as to ask for a car or a rabbit-coat. You've merely asked me to abandon completely every idea and opinion that was ingrained in me since the earliest days in the Colonel's nursery and at my horrible prep school. But don't be disappointed, my love, you have asked a high price. A highish price.' He looked at her, oddly not with the drunken truculence which the mood inspired, but with the same steady sad gaze. Then he ended: 'The drama of demand finishes, inevitably, when the price is paid. Picture me sitting weeping in front of one colleague, one stranger, and one crook with whom, as anybody could guess, my wife is now sleeping. A highish price. But paid. But paid.'

Stella was beginning to sway about, so tired and cold that she could listen to no more. He jumped suddenly to his feet, and said, 'If you want to come in, you'll find the step ladder in the back lavatory. It will enable you to climb to the balcony and thence through the children's room.'

She obeyed his instructions precisely, tearlessly. But in

the children's room she paused, to make sure they were covered up. She had lately insisted that the baby's cot be put in this room after the last feed, lest one night he should be smothered with North German kisses. The boys were fast asleep, looking neither tragic nor at their most beautiful, but higgledy-piggledy and pink. As she came in from the balcony the baby woke. Pausing by the inner door which was ajar, she had a word with him. She bent down by the cot, saying, 'It's all your fault. So it is, it's nobody else's. You started this thing, what with the christening and making me feel like a frump. It's inescapably, directly, primarily your fault, Jacob J.' The baby seemed pleased by the trouble he had caused. He smiled back and looked mystified if not sad, when Stella stood up again, then pulled the door shut, closing out the light.

As she arrived at the bedroom door, Andrew came out to the landing, carrying a blanket and pillow and the pot of whitewash. As he brushed past her on his way downstairs she tried to stop him, asking, 'What the heck are you doing to the place, anyway? Redecorating?'

'No. Disinfecting it.'

Part Three

Part Three

Chapter 17

She did not look much different when George met her a few weeks after his return from Maraschino-land. If anything, she looked more her old self, not less. A button had come off her suède coat and her flat-heeled shoes were as dirty as any student's. Our defences are deeper than we guess. She acknowledged, in a way, the hits which Andrew had scored, but she still talked as much, in the same confusing circles, displaying herself, then contradicting the description, only to present a final picture which was more false than the first. And George was bad for her at this point. Lovingly applauding her shadow-boxing this afternoon, he ill-prepared her for an evening when for the first time in her life she was to feel, fair and square, the thud of an opponent's blow.

The City tea-shop looked like a public lavatory. The walls were tiled, mainly white, but with a line of designed ones depicting in blue Delft, Leiden, and windmills by the Zuider Zee. The waitresses were coloured girls, thin and young and long-armed, wandering about like puppets that had not yet been pulled fully together into their starting position. They cleared the dirty dishes, but in the first place the customers collected their tea from the counter where another girl splashed it recklessly into twenty cups at a time.

George and she sat at a corner table, indulging themselves with sugar which came wrapped in lumps. The chairs round the table were higgeldy-piggeldy and

George, with what can only now be called the constipated air of a Lutheran martyr, piled plates and cups and swept aside the debris left by the previous occupants. There were no tables for less than half-a-dozen people, but most people came to this restaurant alone, or at most with one friend, so the room was only a quarter full when every table was occupied. George had been to the barber lest the idle habits of Maraschino-land should corrupt him. He wore an old and smelly macintosh. He sat, then, stirring his tea, a sweet smile lighting up his lantern of a face as he listened patiently to Stella saying for the third time, 'But there's every reason why I've got to apologise.'

'None.'

'– And explain, of course there is. . . . For heaven's sake.'

'No.'

'George, I mean it, I'm determined. I'm going to explain.'

'I'm not worried, Stella – it doesn't matter: you were in a proper panic, you came a hundred miles to see me. All I did was ring up one bloke I happened to know was searching for Andrew's type – or something like it, and then I forget all about it and go back and play rounders on the sands. If Philbrook takes him it's his business from then on, whatever happens. . . . You're not indebted: you are not under any obligation: I am not hurt or offended.'

Stella sighed. She had one hand in her coat pocket. She said, 'This is really frightening when you start giving me the old good manners. What are you saying behind my back, George?'

'I am saying you're a lovely looking girl. I always have.' He waited a few seconds, then he grinned and made a wide, appealing gesture. 'Be fair, please – what's wrong with the way I'm treating you anyway? Here I am, smiling at everybody, buying you a cup of tea, telling you you're a dish. . . .'

'But there's every reason why I've got to apologise.'

'None.'

'– And explain. Of course there is. Cousin, I'll never have the nerve to ask you a favour again unless we get this straight. You go to a lot of trouble, find a job, and my husband, bless his sweet little heart, takes it, then does nothing but draw the pay and run up expenses. One month later, perfectly rightly, he gets the sack. That's not good for your name, never mind his.'

'Forget it.'

'I won't. D'you think I'm the most ungrateful cow in London? Do you? . . . I'm going to explain.'

He touched his head. 'You're building little things in here. You're imagining.'

She shook her head slowly, and they looked at each other for a moment, George still smiling – 'be fair'. But Stella stared at him very hard and seriously.

'I've rung you four times.'

'Stella, I've not been back long, I've got papers this high on –'

'If I hadn't come and dragged you out of your office you wouldn't be here now.' She sat forward for a moment and drank her tea. An elderly, well-preserved man sitting two tables away gave her a long look as much as to say 'nobody knows anything about bed except me, my dear, you and I could really touch the heights', and slowly, of George, she asked, 'Is this place always filled with sex maniacs?'

'Always,' George confirmed. 'It goes with insurance of all sorts, especially Life.'

But she was back on the subject, at once. She explained, 'I *am* the most ungrateful cow in London, dear. It's me, not Andrew, to blame. He was keen on Philbrook and the Fund and all that. He would have done a good job. Only, various things happened.'

George groaned. 'Fair enough. It doesn't matter, Stella. Philbrook has to find somebody else, so what? He's not a close chum of mine anyway.' He always talked secretively, glancing from time to time, in a hostile way, at nearby tables. Stella did not seem to be listening.

'You bastard,' she said at last. Her eyes looked very dark. 'I thought anything that was my concern was yours, and the other way too. I thought that was one sure thing –'

'Stella,' he checked her, 'if I'm not as happy as I'm pretending to look it's for one reason. We pride ourselves on an honest relationship. You can't expect me to take an interest when you don't tell me the truth.'

'It wasn't Sarson who got this new job for him.'

George took a sip of tea and did not reply. She had one shoulder forward as if she was forced, literally, to skirt the truth. 'You don't believe that?'

'It's not my business, Stella, unless you want it to be.'

'It was Alisdair fixed it. Fixed it with the partners in this other thing –'

'I'm not even sure what this other thing is.'

Stella was too good a self-deceiver to fail to recognise deception in other people. She said, 'You mean what's

Andrew's new firm? . . . Oh, yes, you bloody well do know, George MacNaughten.'

'Somebody said it was stockbroking.'

'Then somebody was right. Did somebody also say that Stella Vass was sleeping with J. T. Sarson?'

He rode it very calmly. 'Nobody other than Stella Vass.'

'When?'

'When you lied, on a beach.'

'Was it obvious?'

'Yes.'

'Is that why you haven't answered the 'phone?'

'Yes.'

'Will you answer the 'phone now I've told you?'

'Yes.'

'Then this has been a good meeting.'

He sniffed and she picked up the sugar bowl and made a little mah-jongg wall with the wrapped lumps.

'It was Alisdair that fixed the job.'

'So you said.'

'Do you believe me?'

'If you say so.'

'I'm finished with Sarson. I was finished with him before Andrew started behaving like this. That's life, isn't it? When I was seeing Sarson, Andrew was as sweet as pie to me: since I stopped he's been really hysterical. He's locked me out of the house, once. He hasn't touched me, sexually I mean, but I'm not asking for sympathy. I'm just stating an ugly fact. Like the other ugly one, that I'm now a stockbroker's moll.'

She took a quick gulp of tea, then more loudly, even wildly, went on, 'Mind you, I say it with a blush, but it's only fair to add that there are stockbrokers and stockbrokers. There's ninety-nine per cent blokes with hot tips, one per cent who actually work it out and go and look at industry and all that. . . . Do I sound as limp as I think I sound?'

'You're talking perfectly good sense. It's true enough –'

She interrupted, thoughtlessly, '. . . I know what you're saying to yourself, George MacNaughten. I know exactly. . . . He's a stockbroker, let's leave it at that.' She almost dived back into her teacup and she replaced it clumsily as if her co-ordination had been affected by the past few weeks' events. George, on the other hand, sat in a collected way, with the springy calm of an experienced male nurse. He suggested comfortingly:

'There's no crime in being a stockbroker's wife.'

She ignored this. She was using a little inhaler to keep her nose and throat clear, though oddly enough there had been no recurrence of the asthma since the night of the hermaphrodite. She said, 'It was Alisdair; it wasn't Sarson who made the contact.'

'Nobody is accusing you.'

'Yes they are!' she yelled back in his face so loudly that he looked all around, guiltily. Then came the swift Red Queen's logic, 'I'm here to excuse myself, therefore, somebody's accusing me, and if you're not then you're not a friend. I don't love you.' She touched his hand as she said that. It was almost as if little crackling sparks dashed off her finger tips, her tension was so great. But she seemed to be unaware of this dishonesty. As he watched her she took her hand away and pushed the inhaler back in her handbag.

194

She said, with a sad little laugh, 'I think I'd rather say I was a lavatory attendant's wife, but it was me who fixed it with Alisdair. I went to him, you see, all brave and on my own, in my leather coat on a summery day, like Himmler's widow with a Glasgow accent, and I insisted on seeing him. He works alone now in the room which used to have a label saying Andrew Vass. You wouldn't have recognised me. I was like someone in a television play, or more like a wartime film. I looked serious and I felt serious and I knew what I wanted and I asked for what I wanted, and after a bit I got what I wanted, and there's a moral tale. If you act like a war widow, they give you widow's benefits. Even when I came out, I was so taken in by the dialogue upstairs that I couldn't see what had happened. Honestly. You haven't met this Alisdair, but he's the monitor or prefect or whatever it is one always hoped would look after one. He's everything that uninspired justice can ask for: fair, slow to anger, never to perceive. . . .'

'I think I see him.'

'He's nice looking, mind.'

'In a grey suit?'

'That's it. *Tending* to wear a grey suit. One of the new, new men, you know? The ones who *tend to think* and *feel surely*, all in Gaitskellian manner, but the result of their deliberations does not permit them to vote Left. Nor Right. . . . Our Alisdair is bang in the middle of this group and he's so plausible that after half an hour you begin to drink it all in. It's really shaming, but I suppose I'm wed to them now. Anyway, we had this grand lunch on a gin and a voucher in one of those downstairs dining-rooms a lot smarter than this, filled with young men like him. So much so that I felt under terrible compulsion to yell at the top of my voice, "Sarson's a big stoat, I've got reason to know." '

George cringed. 'And did you? '

'No, I'm telling you. I got swallowed up by them. I listened and replied and all that while he talked about the most effective job that we could effect for Andrew effectively, as if this was what life was all about – squeezing curved pieces into square holes like I.C.I. and Helen's Court and that. I start thinking like this, too, adding up Andrew's pluses and marking minus for each drawback. It didn't even occur to me then to take a grip of his hand and say, "Look, dear boy, whether Andrew's all plus or all minus, executive-wise, could not be less relevant – you've got an obligation to go out and find him something, because Andrew is weak and Andrew is hurt and worse still, sorry for himself." '

She stopped suddenly, and blushed, but it was impossible to tell whether she felt ashamed of her dishonesty or her disloyalty. She stared at him silently for a moment, then she began again, 'Imagine it, Alisdair and me as chums. . . . I see things his way exactly, suspend my belief in life and think like him that the future lies in a close understanding of Keynesian economics and the preservation of a modest manner. Shallow enough, but at that time it was refreshing and a relief to talk to someone who was at least prepared to be constructive. Within twenty-four hours we're having a second meeting and I'm drinking in all this spiel about the new stockbrokers being a different breed from those at which my grandad spat, even at the risk of the five pound penalty. Alisdair puts it very nicely, about Investment Consultants in the States being half-way between the stockbroker and the merchant bank. With great anxiety and fine thin features, because he's getting more serious every hour, he says, "This is right for Andrew," and there am I, starry-eyed, saying, "Oh, yes, yes, yes. This is, surely." Mind, to understand all this fully you should know the chaos there is in the home, just at this time, with one room half redecorated, Elsa giving in her notice, Bill Williams buying phenobarbitone pills and putting them down the lavatory pan, glasses needing washing, children needing talking to and Andrew taking pay from the Fund and never leaving home at all. Just telling me, now and then, to get the ice from the fridge. Chaos. I don't joke, George. I may laugh at the grey suit, but Alisdair Pitt, at this point, is like a knight in shining armour and I'm saying all the time, "If only we can get Andrew employed, that's all. I ask for nothing else!" It's unemployment with a new twist, this, but it's equally distressing.'

She was chain smoking. 'I'm coming up to the big reunion scene, the big triumph of my life. When I finally kick Jimmy Maxton in the teeth.'

'I can guess,' George quietly replied. 'When Andrew gets the job.'

'He gets the letter first, and there's a new look in his eye. What's really awful is that even at that point I don't see how far I'm selling out.'

'There's no good carrying a banner, Stella, if there's children starving at home. No, be fair – I'm sorry to give you the old Daddy talk, but there's such a thing as coming to terms with life. Of marrying the old ideals and necessities. That's all you've done.'

She shoved her cup over and silently, but again with his most encouraging, kindest smile, George walked over to the counter and took two new cups, with the tea overflowing into the saucers.

'I'm going to go on,' she said, 'I want to go on. I want to remember the moment I thought was the real triumph, truly, George, the triumph of my life. The moment he came in through the door, I knew fine we were in, we were there. It wasn't a new man. It was Andrew as I first knew him. Andrew with the excitement bursting out of him like it can with nobody else. Andrew saying yes, yes, yes. Andrew with a hand out to me and everybody else he ever set eyes on, the bloody baby he is –' Her throat sounded sore as she said more calmly, 'We stand there like a couple surprised by their own proposals, like a couple of bean-poles planted too close. My face is getting rounder and rounder and all of a sudden – suddenly, now, I just burst out crying.'

She paused, half smiled, and continued on a high note, 'He's very sweet, and predictable, and it was smoked salmon he had brought back which we ate later, on the woolly rug. And I knew he was young enough to forget all the Bill Williams stuff and that he needn't end up with all the other neurotics, with booze and pills and moans. He'll not be a boring zombie, he'll be a boring City bore, and he'll be talking about the fourth of June and inside information in the City, and, George . . .'

Tears suddenly began to pour down her cheeks. 'And I'm lying, I'm lying, George. . . . I'm telling you what I hope's going to happen one of these nights. I'm not telling you the truth at all. . . . Christ,' she added as she caught her sobs, 'even the sex maniacs are doubting now.' She tried to laugh as the man opposite pulled on his coat and hurried away.

George was calming her and at the same time trying to find out where the lies ended, and where they began. The limits she admitted were clear.

'He got the letter, that's true,' she said. 'He got the job, that's also true. He's doing it well. Alisdair says he's back to the old vital form, in the City. The scene on the rug to the accompaniment of smoked salmon is what is called wishful thinking. Which is horrible and shows you the state I'm in.'

George could only say, 'It'll happen sooner or later. Probably sooner than you know.' Then he added, 'You sound as if you still love him.'

She laughed bitterly and said, 'Don't you remember, I sounded as if I loved Jimmy Maxton and all his works? And there you are. I've utterly succeeded in betraying both.' She sighed and combed back her hair. She snapped shut her handbag which she wore over her shoulder like a school satchel. Then she stood up, abruptly, clearly determined to finish the tea-party, at once. She looked straight, and thin, and beautiful.

'But it's done now, son. I just came to say don't think you're the only one who's saying "somewhere along the line, she's eaten of that apple!"'

She did not recognise then how successful she had been in achieving her objective. George was almost on his knees.

'Stella, I'm not saying that. I would never blame you. You're right – you're a wife, first – you –'

But she was on her way. She did not hear him. She

199

gave a bright little laugh, and a hard one. She said, 'No comments, dear, I'll be seeing you. No flowers, please. I'm quite prepared for what's coming to me,' she added, so wrongly. 'Didn't you hear? All socialists like us are insecure and to cure that there's nothing like a real dose of insecurity.'

'Stella –'

But nothing would stop her. Buttoning her coat she ran upstairs and squeezed through the bunch of secretaries queuing for bread. She swung through the glass doors on to the crowded, narrow City pavement, where pale clerk-wristed men were already buying evening papers on their way to suburban trains.

Chapter 18

An unwritten sub-title to the Radcliffe Report on the
Bank of England might be 'What the hell should a
chap do on Wednesday afternoon?' The Bank Rate is
announced on Thursdays. Any change is decided, therefore, by the Assembled Court at their Wednesday meeting. When change is in the air a Director can therefore
do nothing right, elsewhere in the City, that afternoon.
To answer yes or no is to lie or tell the truth, both of
which are harmful. To fail to answer is equally dangerous; it is to make an illicit suggestion. But this Wednesday, the same day on which Stella met her cousin
George in the tea-shop, Sarson did not even attend the
luncheon. He was following up another interest on
behalf of the same firm which had bought the Glasgow
concern. That the Germans were determined people was
no news; that Alisdair was still coping with their prob-
lems was public knowledge. He constantly complained
about it. But that the Germans might, at once, be con-
sidering expanding their British interests, by buying yet
another British concern (this time in Luton) was known
only by three people – Alisdair, Miss Parker and Sarson
– and suspected by one. Andrew after all, was the only
other person familiar with the Germans' ambitions as
they had stated them at the early conferences. And he
had not forgotten them.

But Andrew had not left Copthall Avenue when his
wife arrived home that evening. It was the new foreign
girl, a Norwegian, who met Stella in the hall and an-

nounced Sarson's presence. She did so with a knowing look. At seventeen she had ideas below her station, believing hopefully that south of Bergen all the world was a brothel.

Stella did not even take off her coat. Stuffing her beret in her pocket, she walked slowly to the sitting-room, undoing her buttons as she went.

Sarson was on his hands and knees playing with David, Josh and a company of toy soldiers. When Stella came in, he did not at once rise to his feet but continued to form up the ranks on the unpolished linoleum at the edge of the carpet. The boys were obviously delighted with their visitor. They said so to their mother as she dismissed them, kindly but firmly. Slowly, then, Sarson rose to his feet, looking altogether too big and too grand for the crowded little room. As the children left he spoke of them, with a mild smile.

He said, 'Had I been better acquainted with my protégés I would have been altogether more diligent in furthering their education. I wonder if you ever wrote to that housemaster?'

Because he looked so big and wrong there she seemed uncomfortable. It was too cold and late to walk in the garden. The grass was soaking wet, the path muddy. To close the door would have been to exaggerate the smallness of the room. Cramped in the corner by the open door she said, 'This place never looked more dreadful. There's not room to swing a cat in here.'

He made one of his heavy little jokes. 'Are we swinging?'

She answered, 'I suppose yours was the Rolls down the road there. I never even noticed the number.'

'It isn't significant.' He said, 'I haven't yet descended to J.T.S. 1.'

'There isn't any other room.'

'Is this so bad?' Stooping down, he placed the sergeant of toy soldiers at the end of the front rank. He said, 'I'm not sure if he shouldn't be in the front. . . .' Then looking round he added, 'It seems quite cosy to me.'

'Thank you, dear,' she replied. 'You big hypocritical puss.'

She went across to the mantelpiece where she found one stale cigarette in a broken bamboo box. She asked him, as she lit it, 'What the hell are you doing here, anyway?' Then before he could answer she said, 'If by any chance you're here for what I think you're here for, you'd better know that our little run-around's over. The wedding's off, dear, if that's why you've called.'

Sarson grinned and ran his fingers through his hair. He was too wise a man to pretend any authority off his own ground. He brought all the other weapons into play, instead; the boyishness, the humour, the shyness, the reasonableness – the whole, irresistible charm.

'What's so wonderful about you,' he said, 'is that you always answer your own questions, even when you do so backside foremost. But if you want to know, I'm here because I'm rather hurt.'

'I'll believe it.'

'You know why.'

'Because I haven't answered your 'phone calls?'

'That as well.' He sat down on the arm of the mock leather, which was the best of the chairs. 'But more

203

than that, with reason. Surely? I didn't have to tell you that if you were in some sort of fix I was always here. Did that really have to be underlined?'

'You mean about Andrew's job?'

'Of course. To go to Alisdair like that – of course I would have helped. By going to him you're passing terrible judgements on me.' He watched her very carefully. She had thrown off her coat and now sat down on a stool by the empty fireplace. She smoked hard, in her Bloomsbury pose.

'I'm sorry if I offended you. But not to worry.'

'Everything's fixed up?'

She looked at him hard and he went on gently, 'I am glad.'

'If you mean "Am I now a stockbroker's wife?",' she said with considerable, almost lesbian hostility, 'the answer is "Yes". If you look carefully you can see the oak beams in my eye.'

He didn't think much of that, as a joke. He said, 'I can hear the bitterness in your voice, anyway.'

'Do you blame me?'

Slowly, he chuckled, his hand to his hair once more. 'Well, yes, I think I do.'

'That's because you wouldn't understand what selling out means. The joke about the oak beams has only come up the second week. The first, when I twigged just what I'd done, I couldn't speak at all.'

Sarson was harder. 'And just what had you done?'

'I'd fixed myself, dear heart, to live the rest of my life in direct conflict with what I believe.'

He hardened again, on that, asking coldly, 'Weren't you doing that when you were sleeping with me?'

She sighed. 'The point is that I'm no longer sleeping with you.'

'So now you're getting the worst of both worlds.'

'More or less.'

Sarson rose. 'Well, I must say that does sound ludicrous. I'm not quite sure whether I'm meant to sympathise or –'

'You're meant to write me off.'

'As a girl-friend?'

She blew smoke down her nose. 'As a bloke,' she said, and he laughed again.

'But it's amazing,' he said. 'The situation seems to me to be precisely what it was a few months ago when you came bouncing up to my flat, all wind, windy and winded. No please –' he added, as she tried to interrupt, 'don't for God's sake start gassing when you look so pretty sulking. You'll only give yourself asthma, as you have done before – and, alas, love, as you will do again, unless somebody bonks you on the nose and stops you going round in giddy circles.' He pouted. 'Not that it's the nose that's uppermost in my mind.'

'Just let me say –'

'Nothing will I let you say. Not until you've listened to me for at least two minutes. I told you I came here in the first place because I was disappointed.'

'Liar.'

'On the contrary, I merely refrained from telling you the extent of my disappointment.'

As usual the nastiest blows came in a soft, almost vague tone.

'I'm afraid I mean it severely. Your opinion of yourself is a highish one, all considered. Since I came into

205

your life you have been unfaithful to your husband and paid the terrible price of winding up in circumstances where you're going to be the hell of a lot richer than you might expect, but in a situation in which it will be difficult for you to sit astride strange rich men, singing, defiantly, the Red Flag. I merely wish to point out that you've changed nothing. When you came to me in the flat you were saying exactly the same thing, only putting it in a different tense, namely the future. You weren't going to sleep with me, because your scruples, of the most curious and muddled politico-moral order, prevented you from doing so, the implication being frankly jingoistic, "I'm not going to sleep with you, dear, but by jingo if I do." Consider your actions, coolly, and you will find that absolutely nothing has changed. You're up to the same old tricks. In the course of the last two weeks you have done the following things. You have sent, if indirectly, wild alarms to me by enrolling the help of a son-in-law quite famous for his indiscretion. You have re-employed your husband in anti-red flag land. You have told me, here, within a matter of seconds, dramatically and almost with those easy, easy tears of yours, that you have decided to live your life in conflict, which is to say frankly that you still haven't come to any conclusion whatsoever.'

The Norwegian girl re-entered at this point, asking Stella if she should make some coffee or tea, staring all the time at Sarson who looked her over in a way that made Stella blush with anger. But as soon as she retired he again raised his hand, to stop Stella from speaking, and himself continued, 'We are speaking, if you haven't recognised it, about crooks and hypocrites, fast progressing to the conclusion that the second category – apart from containing all the world's idiots – also encompasses the worst shits.'

He smiled, happily, 'Once, I remember, at some aggravatingly inopportune moment you told me about my immorality – admitting, of course, in the same un-controlled breath, that it was no worse than your own, though I thought then, as I think now, that you were kind to yourself. You sang, again rather typically, not the Red Flag, as you like to see yourself doing, but "Give me my bow of burning gold", a sentiment with which I am, by temperament, altogether less in sympathy. But perhaps the tune is easier. At any rate you asked me – prompted, I guess, by an earlier discussion about my wife's country life – if I would ever dare fall in love with a girl with a mind. I answered "yes" and you kissed me so tenderly that I refrained from adding what was strongly in my head, namely that it quite amazed me that I could become so attached to someone without a mind. You, my love. . . . For the purpose of a mind is to calculate odds, come to a decision and act upon it, a process which I have never yet seen you complete. . . . Don't cry,' he added suddenly, seeing her face, 'but if you must, don't pretend that you do so in anger when you so clearly do so in shame.'

But the tears came, just the same. She said, 'It's ex-haustion, nothing else.'

'That I can believe, but it can be cured very simply. Just stop running round in circles with a "Ban the Bomb" on the front of your banner, and "Kick me, ducky" on the back.'

She said, 'You're jilting me, aren't you?' and for the first time, it stopped his flow.

He crossed over to where she sat and took both her hands, and looked at her very hard. He said, 'You are such an idiot. If you can work that out so swiftly why couldn't you have done the rest?'

'I don't know,' she said hopelessly, 'I'm stuck. Somewhere I got stuck.'

'Not any more,' he replied, and after a while he stood up and sighed, and with his hands on his hips looked down at her.

'You are so pretty, too,' he said. 'But darling, such an ass.'

'Why couldn't I have met someone like you at the start?'

'Because I wouldn't have married you.'

'Now you're just kicking me in the teeth.'

'That's rather how decisions seem to work out,' he said vaguely, then scratched his head. 'I want to make a 'phone call, by the way.'

'It's in the hall,' she said, and he went back to her for a second, and stooped over her.

She said, 'Please can I ask a girlish question?'

'Yes.'

'Does all this mean you love me?'

'Objection,' he replied very kindly. 'That's not a girlish question. It's a childish one.' Then rather stiffly, protesting that he was getting too old for girls, he stretched his back straight and wandered out of the room.

When she had patched herself up, staring at herself in the dark mirror on the dresser and scarcely preventing herself from breaking out in tears again, she came through to the hall to find him still talking on the 'phone. She quickly recognised to whom he was speaking when she heard him say, 'It's whatever you want, my dear, but I would have thought it much simpler from Salmon's point of view if you were to leave the Mini at the station down there.' He gave a little groan, half turned to smile to Stella, as the bright hoo-ray voice at the other end contradicted him, then confused the arrangements again.

They were standing like this, looking at each other, when there was the noise of a key in the front-door and Andrew, looking bright, but paler and slimmer in a new dark suit, walked in.

Stella, for a moment, looked panic-stricken, but Sarson did not seem to be perturbed. 'I'm so sorry, Andrew,' he said, putting his hand on the mouthpiece. 'Jennifer's moving us all over the place. I don't know what Salmon's going to say.'

'He just dropped in,' Stella said, unhappily.

Sarson supported her. 'Passing by.' Then he turned back again to repeat his latest orders of march for the week-end.

Andrew flung his folded evening paper on the oak chest at the bottom of the stairs and kissed his wife, briskly, on the cheek; then he turned back to Sarson, who, at last, replaced the receiver.

Andrew said, 'I saw the car outside.' Sarson was going through his pockets. He said wearily, 'I'd better write all this down. . . . You must excuse me using you as a public 'phone box. I've been playing toy soldiers with your sons.'

Andrew said, 'Who won?'

Sarson looked embarrassed for a moment. 'I'm most awfully sorry,' he said. 'I'm afraid I don't know how much the cost of a call to –'

'Forget it,' Andrew said. 'You heard I'm fixed up in the Stock Exchange?' Sarson's reactions seemed abnormally slow. In this alone did he betray his surprise at the change in his former assistant. Most noticeable were the dropping of the 'sir', and the paleness of the cheeks. The pink in them had vanished.

'I congratulated Stella,' Sarson said.

'Huh!' Andrew quickly replied. 'Didn't she tell you it was against her principles? You on your way back?'

'That's it,' Sarson said. 'I've had a lousy day in the Midlands.'

'Where was that?' Andrew asked and Sarson looked at his bright eyes.

'Birmingham!' he said at last, getting into his coat as Stella opened the door.

Andrew looked enormously pleased with himself. He said, 'That's funny, Salmon said Luton,' and Sarson replied, 'Oh did he?' as if it were the sort of mistake he made every day.

Outside, he paused on the front step and at once the big Rolls moved up to the gate. Stella was biting her lip. Then as he moved off, Sarson turned back and pointed to the plant by the step. He said, 'That magnolia ought to be tied up,' and as if she were being left in school she said, 'Yes, yes,' and nodded violently.

She stood on the step as the Rolls moved off and she waved it on its way, to Highgate, Whittington's Hill, to the City with its new buildings, and its old cries. Sarson looked calm but serious, reading his paper, in the back seat.

The end, or the beginning, came very swiftly.

When she went back into the hall she had started to explain that she had been out when Sarson first called. She was excusing herself even before she closed the door. She swore she had not rung him and pleaded that Andrew should believe and trust her. But, on the 'phone himself now, to his colleagues in the City, trying to place an after-hours sale, Andrew did not heed her. As she talked and talked he totally ignored her, although he was waiting for several minutes for a second colleague to come to the 'phone. Then he made another, similar call. Still she spoke. Still he did not reply.

Andrew seemed to have no interest in Sarson's reasons for calling, his actions in the house or the duration of his stay. The only significance, which greatly excited him, was that Sarson had arrived from Luton. His colleagues were obviously as pleased as he was. They were going to back his hunch with big money, and Andrew was an equal partner in the deal. He was in.

At last he replaced the receiver, to find Stella silent, at the other end of the hall. She stood in the shadows, her feet apart, white-faced, staring at him as if she would be insulted no more. He had kept her waiting like that for almost ten minutes, but he had no intention of apologising. He too stood still, his hands behind him on the sill where the telephone stood. For a long, long time, they remained like this, fixed and hostile, like brother and sister hoarse and naked in the back street; which is to say, reduced to that blazing attachment where passion starts.

When will you pay me?
Say the Bells of Old Bailey.
When I grow rich,
Say the Bells of Shoreditch.